The Tears of a Cowboy

Crossroads Creek Cowboys

Elsie Davis

Sweet Romance Publishing

Cover Design by getcovers.com

Edited by Elaine Hyatt (Clarity Editing Services)

Edited by Cassandra Cornell

Sweet Romance Publishing

Sweetromancepublishing.com

PO Box 778

Liberty, NC 27298

Ephesians 4:32
*"Be kind and compassionate to one another,
forgiving each other, just as in Christ God
forgave you."*

Chapter One

❤

"Captain Liam Carter reporting for duty, sir," undercover Texas Ranger Ben Calhoun said, rapping his knuckles against Chief Jackson's open office door. He spied a coffee machine on a shelf in the corner, the aroma of fresh brew calling his name since he didn't have the foresight to stop at the Super Saver Grocery store when he arrived in Crossroads Creek yesterday.

"Come in, come in. I was expecting you a little earlier than this," the chief said as he stood, glancing at his watch. He was a portly, balding man, older than Ben expected, with kind eyes that contradicted his gruff demeanor.

Ben pulled back, a little surprised at being called out for a ten-minute delay on his first day. Either the chief was a stern taskmaster, or he wasn't happy about Ben's presence. It wouldn't take long to figure out which. "Sorry. I was getting settled in at the new place and familiarizing myself with the layout. My boss, Ranger Chief Wilcox, speaks highly of you, and I know you've been fully briefed on the situation," Ben said, dropping his voice a notch. He closed the door behind him and moved closer to the oversized desk that consumed the office. Ben wouldn't be asking for a cup of coffee now since he had already irritated his new temporary boss.

The chief shot a glance toward the wall of glass windows that gave him a view of his entire department personnel in action. Sunlight brightened the workspace as it streamed through the windows. The chief turned back to Ben. "The walls have ears." He stood and came round the desk, offering his hand in welcome.

"Gotcha, sir." Ben understood the need for secrecy. The chief didn't want him in Crossroads Creek, but that made two of them. Returning to the place where he grew up, a place where every street corner whispered accusations about the tragic accident that ripped his world apart wasn't on his priority list. Though it's not like he was given the choice of turning down the undercover case.

"Let's drop the formalities for a moment and cut to the chase, Ben. You are here because Chief Wilcox, Larry—is my friend, and this is a favor to him. I can't begin to explain the problems associated with you getting the promotion to captain in my department, but it was no small task. That being said, I want the kidnappers caught as much as everyone else does. The fact that they kidnapped a child fifteen miles from here and in Tumbleweed County has everyone shaken up. So, ultimately, I'm all for the Texas Rangers investigating these cases." The chief leaned back in his leather chair, a thoughtful expression on his face.

"I'll do my best to put an end to this kidnapping ring. You've read my dossier. There can be no slip ups. I'm Captain Liam Carter moving forward, and it would be best if, from this point forward, we don't use my real name."

The chief nodded. "I sure hope no one recognizes you. I wasn't here when you were a boy, but lots of folks in town have excellent memories."

"Doubtful." Ben chuckled, though the sound held little humor. "The long-haired trouble maker and problem child of Crossroads Creek has long been forgotten. I'm sure it was a case of good riddance. It's been twenty years since I've been here. And anyone that might have remembered me won't recognize me anyway as I was a dark brown-haired boy then, and not sporting the cool sandy-blond hair I have now."

The chief nodded. "Good. Sergeant Peters is going to blow a fuse when she doesn't get the promotion she's expecting. I hope you're prepared to deal with the hurricane about to hit this office when she finds out."

"I'm accustomed to handling the toughest cases and the tough people that go with them, so I'm sure I can handle her. It's only for three weeks." Ben shifted his weight, aware that his words might sound arrogant, but they were simply the truth. Texas Rangers got the job done, and he worked harder and longer than anyone else in his department Though in part because he didn't do relationships that would divide his time with the Rangers. He was married to his job. Anything else would be too complicated, not to mention too dangerous.

"See that you do. I don't believe for a second that Sergeant Peters can't be trusted. Otherwise, I wouldn't be making her captain once you leave," the chief added, staring him down to make a point.

And Ben agreed—on the surface. "I'm sure you're right, but until I've ruled her out as a suspect, she's still on the list. There's got to be someone on the inside helping the kidnappers, and it's my job to figure out who." Ben would dot his I's and cross his T's to make sure everything was done by the book, just as his professional training demanded. With eight unsolved kidnappings in the last six years, and all of them within a triangulated area, including Austin, Dallas, and Abilene, something had to give. With the last one happening in Wylie, his boss, Ranger Chief Wilcox had landed Ben in Crossroads Creek for this investigation.

"I won't say anything. Just don't make her any madder than she's already going to be. I'll need her when you're gone. She's one of the most dedicated police officers I've known over the years. Doesn't date. Just works."

More information that's good to know. "She sounds a lot like me, so we'll have something in common. I'm certain there are several operatives within the region, but if I can just find one, it might be the break we need to put an end to this kidnapping ring."

"I trust the people you work for have sent the best they've got. Do your job and let me do mine. That's all I ask. This is my town, and I've got good officers working for me. And for the record, I don't believe for a minute anyone from this department is involved."

"Fair enough, but I'm here to check out all the police departments in the vicinity near Wylie, not just Crossroads Creek. Please keep that in mind. It's not targeted at any one department." Ben hoped the man was right. Law enforcement officers were a tight-knit group and were a whole lot less likely to accept him as a rookie officer, hence the need to make him their boss.

"Then we are on the same page. Your desk is the one in the back right corner. We don't have many fancy offices in our building. Morning briefing starts sharply at eight-fifteen." Chief Jackson nodded, picking up his phone to signal the end of their conversation.

Chapter Two

♥

"SO, TODAY'S THE BIG day?" Jenna asked, her best friend's early morning call giving Mandy cause to smile. The two became best friends when Mandy moved to Crossroads Creek four years ago.

It was nice that her friend remembered the significance of today and cared. "It is. After eight years of hard work and determination working as a police officer, it's my time to shine. Chief Jackson has all but guaranteed me the captain's promotion," Mandy added. Eight years and a lot of tears. She absently touched the cross pendant at her neck.

"I can't think of anyone who deserves it more. Let's meet up tonight and celebrate.

Maybe at Radcliff's in Fontana, and then we can go dancing."

Jenna's enthusiasm was contagious, but Mandy would still have to draw the line. "It's Monday and I have to work tomorrow morning. Maybe we can do dinner and wait for the weekend to do any official celebrations that include dancing and staying out late."

"Sounds good, but I'm going to hold you to it. You never like to go out. All work and no play makes Mandy a dull girl."

Gee, thanks. My determination to rise to the top in my department in a career dominated by men has been the focus I needed over the years. It was that or lose myself in grief. I'm the way I am for survival. You know all this. Hold on a minute." Mandy laid the phone on the arm of the sofa. She pulled on her work boots, thinking over what Jenna said.

It hadn't always been this way for her. Once upon a time she planned to become a lawyer working in Austin, where she was born and raised and never planned to leave. But then her parents died in a car accident, and not long after that, the rest of her life went terribly wrong, spinning out of control. It was then she made the career change to go into law enforcement and joined the Austin PD.

Only Jenna knew the whole truth. Well, almost the whole truth. There was still one detail Mandy hadn't shared with anyone. At least, not anyone outside the case of her missing daughter.

She checked the time, realizing she needed to hustle it up. It wouldn't do to be late for this morning's briefing. She picked the phone up. "Sorry, I was putting on my boots."

"Mandy, I do know how hard you've worked, and I'm sorry for my careless remark. I'm not trying to make you feel guilty, but I just want you to lighten up and live life again. Hopefully, the captain's promotion will be the validation you need and then you can let up a bit. Meet someone new. Your ex-husband was a class-A jerk to leave you, especially knowing the ordeal you were going through. He wasn't the right guy, just saying. But someone out there will be perfect for you."

Mandy double-checked the safety on her Ruger and holstered it, securing the strap over the handle. The familiar weight of the weapon brought her comfort, not that she'd ever had to use it. She grabbed her wallet off the table in the hall before heading for the door. "I know and I agree. With the class-A jerk part, not the someone for me part. The fact that John and his second wife had a baby girl was like a slap upside the head. It was a harsh reality that life doesn't always work out the way we think is fair. On top of everything else, that is what hurt so much. But God has seen me through the dark days, and I promise I'm doing better."

"So, you agree it's time to date? It's been eight years, Mandy, and you're only thirty-three."

"I'm well aware of how much time has passed," she said, her voice taking on a wistful tone as she slid into the car. "And I said nothing about dating," Mandy chuckled, pushing the heart-breaking memories aside. "My career will still be my focus. Dating just isn't my thing. My happiness will never be complete without my daughter, or knowing what happened to her. A relationship deserves more commitment than I can give." She glanced at the small angel pin on her visor, a reminder to keep faith. They had this conversation at least once a year, but Mandy's answer never changed.

"I disagree. A good guy will understand the loss you're dealing with. In fact, I may have found you the perfect blind date. Just say yes. Please."

Mandy shook her head. "No. But I'll think about it. I promise. Besides, if he's such a perfect date, why aren't you dating him?"

"Because I'm going on a date with his brother." Jenna laughed.

"Now I understand, but still a no. And if I don't get a move on, I'll be late for work and the chief may give my job to someone else."

She put the car in reverse and backed down the driveway.

"Doubtful. There's no one in the department more deserving than you."

"Thanks, Jenna."

"Okay, so Radcliff's at six, Captain Peters?"

Mandy loved the sound of the official title. "Deal." She hung up the phone, thinking over her best friend's suggestion of a blind date. She simply couldn't bring herself to say yes.

Eight years hadn't lessened the pain in Mandy's heart after her one-week-old daughter had been kidnapped. Nor the resulting divorce after her husband blamed her for their daughter's disappearance. The question remained...could she have done more? Mandy was never charged, but that didn't stop the disapproving stares and questioning looks from the police department.

Their suspicions had run high, and it was only by the grace of God that she'd not been charged with negligence or involvement. But it had been the catalyst for her to change her career path to outright law enforcement, knowing it would give her the best chance to continue her own investigations into the disappearance of her daughter. It was only after four years, when nothing had turned up, that she finally transferred from the Austin PD to the Crossroads Creek PD. A new town and a new life. A chance to start over without all the constant reminders of the past. Of course, she left them a forwarding address and contact information, but no one had ever reached out to her.

The police station loomed ahead, its brick exterior familiar and welcoming. It was after all, like a second home to her. Mandy pulled into the parking lot and made her way into the building, loving the security it brought her. This is where she belonged. Now, more than ever. She noticed no one was at their desks, which could only mean one thing. They were already all in the meeting room for the morning briefing. A meeting in which Chief

Jackson was going to announce the new captain.

Mandy pushed open the door, and all eyes landed on her. The weight of their stares pressed against her chest. She walked to one of the empty chairs, took a seat, and then scanned the sea of officer's faces, unnerved by the eerie silence. Usually, the room was buzzing with conversation. Her gaze landed on the stranger in the room, the guy sitting next to the chief. Sandy-blond hair and the darkest brown eyes to match his dark bushy eyebrows. Sharply chiseled jaw. Lean and broad-shouldered. But it was the guy's plain clothes that reminded her of a city detective on steroids. Like the guys in CSI.

Handsome. Yes, but not classically so. Self-assured. Without a doubt. The man didn't flinch when she stared him down, only giving back as good as she gave. Mandy shifted her focus to the chief as he stood.

"Good morning, Sergeant Peters. Nice of you to show up for the meeting." Chief Jackson's voice was tense and unforgiving, something not called for, as she was never late.

She checked at her watch. Eight-fourteen. One minute to spare—so what was his problem? And who was the stranger? Her jubilation for the upcoming announcement now dimmed, she held back the smart remark on the tip of her tongue. "Thank you, sir. Wouldn't miss this for the world," she said instead, shooting him a warm smile of expectation, while trying to block out the man's face sitting next to him.

Chief Jackson nodded and let out a heavy sigh. "*Umm*, yes. Before we get to the daily briefing, I've got an announcement to make."

Mandy held her breath. This was it. The moment she'd been waiting for. Her heart raced, her throat parched with anticipation.

"As you all know, Captain Thomas left us a few weeks ago. It's time to name his replacement. I want you all to give a warm welcome to Captain Liam Carter, our newest member of the Crossroads Creek Police Department."

The words *Captain Liam Carter* dealt Mandy a sudden blow she hadn't expected, her head spinning as the implications sank in. *She didn't get the job.* Her hand instinctively reached for the cross at her neck, seeking comfort. It took everything she had not to blurt out in anger. Something was drastically wrong here. She struggled to breathe as she reined in her emotions.

Amidst the clapping of the others in the room, she belatedly remembered to join them in the congratulations. Two claps ought to suffice. Questions burned in her mind. Who was this guy? Why did he get her job? The answers would have to wait, but she wouldn't leave today without them. From the chief. Now wasn't the time, but later she'd insist on an explanation. It could be years before she'd have another chance at a promotion. It would seem the job had gone to a man—again.

And not even someone from within the department, adding insult to injury. She said a silent prayer for strength and guidance, knowing she'd need both to face whatever lay ahead.

Chapter Three

❤

LIAM WAS MORE THAN a little aware of the emotional rollercoaster Sergeant Peters was experiencing. The flash of anger was quickly concealed, but not before he had seen it. Duly noted—the chief was right. He shifted in his chair, the weight of his deception heavy on his mind. But then, the officer was expecting a promotion and it had been ripped right out from under her. He felt a slight twinge of remorse, but it was the undercover case that was the most important factor in the way things would play out over the next few weeks. The Texas Rangers were stepping up the investigation, the Wylie kidnapping pushing them to do more.

Just three weeks to follow a hunch after he'd been studying the statewide kidnapping files and discovered a pattern, lumping eight of them as having the same method of operation. The MO included no break-ins, toddlers and young children, at night, and in his opinion, less than stellar efforts to investigate. The kidnappers were careful and covered their tracks well, but it was the hope of the Texas Rangers team that by concentrating on the patterns, they might discover something that would point them in the right direction. *Finally*.

If Liam was wrong, he'd go back to Dallas and pick up a fresh case. Though, in all honesty, he was unlikely to stop working on this one. The more he read the files, the more determined he was to figure out what was going on. Each photo of a missing child stirred something deep within him, a reminder of his sister and the painful memories of her death. More than anything else, he wanted to find the children and return them to their parents.

He stood and forced a smile to his face, taking in the wary expressions of his new team. "Thanks, Chief Jackson. This is quite an honor for sure. I mean, I can't believe I've been given such a huge promotion after such a short time with the police force in Dallas. I'll do my best for the team, but I'll really need someone to show me the ropes here in the country and catch me up to speed. Any volunteers to help a newbie?" he asked, grinning as he scanned the sea of faces whose expressions had turned to shocked disbelief. The plan for him to appear less experienced had been a genius idea by his boss, knowing the other officers in Tumbleweed County wouldn't feel as threatened by the newcomer.

"Exactly what is your experience?" one officer asked, voicing the question in every person's mind.

"Well, I worked the beat as an officer for a year and then I was promoted to sergeant the following year. I took some extra law enforcement classes at a college after my shift. I think that's why I'm being promoted, which is pretty great. I've always looked up to my uncle, who's been a lieutenant with the Dallas PD for a long time. He'll love this. Chip off the old block, so to speak." Liam grinned and ran a hand through his hair, deliberately messing it up. It gave the appearance of someone who didn't care about his personal appearance which would extend itself to a belief his work ethic wouldn't be that focused either.

"Chief Jackson, please tell us this is a joke?" Sergeant Peters spoke up, covering her mouth as though she instantly regretted the words. She flushed red, the color more pronounced with her blue eyes and fair skin.

The chief shook his head and scowled. "No joke." He leaned forward over the table, hands flat against the surface. "And guess what—for that insubordinate remark, you get the honor of partnering with the new guy to show him around and get him up to speed. And make sure you issue him some standard uniforms. My decision is final. And anyone that doesn't like it, tough. Now let's get down to business, shall we?"

Sergeant Peters' eyes narrowed to slits, her lips drawn tight as she fought back a retort.

The chief wanted him to go easy on her, but perhaps he should have taken a page out of his own playbook. Saddling them together probably wasn't the best idea. As the department's best, she would be the one most likely to question his every move. Something he didn't want her doing.

The fluorescent lights hummed overhead as Liam settled back in his seat, not looking forward to the first private meeting the two of them shared. He was, however, pleased with the initial reception he'd received from the others. He needed them to think he was handed a gift with the promotion They might not like it much, but they would be less wary of him.

As the chief went over his notes and handed out assignments, it gave him time to observe his fellow officers. There were only five others besides Peters and the chief. They all seemed like a normal bunch of police officers. Grumbling over boring tasks, hassling each other, and joking about other issues. But overall, a tight-knit group that liked their jobs. If their attitudes were anything to go by, that is. They all pulled patrol shifts, except the chief, that is. A little unusual, but then it would seem they were short staffed, and everyone chipped in to get the job done. Still, the only person in the room he was willing to rule out as a suspect for involvement with the kidnapping ring was the chief himself.

Liam's hunch was that someone in Tumbleweed County law enforcement was involved in the latest kidnapping in Wylie. Being the most recent case, it was the best chance he had to figure out what was going on. His job was to find a weak link and exploit it in order to backtrack through the other cases. The Wylie kidnapping also came up short on the police work end of things, with some leads never followed up. His boss coordinated the set-up of the undercover operation, using Crossroads Creek as a base because of its proximity to Wylie.

And given Liam had grown up here and still owned the ranch where he was staying, it made his cover that much easier to put into place. The current renters had moved to Colorado, and Liam had considered selling the ranch, but now it would have to wait. He'd instructed Terrance, his high school friend and property manager, not to re-rent the house. It had been easy enough for him to become the next *renter*. Terrance was the only one in Crossroads Creek who knew the truth, and it was because of his past connection with the town that led Chief Wilcox to drop the case in his lap. It was meant to be.

When he had arrived, he discovered the ranch house was in dire need of a coat of paint and repairs. The barn doors were sagging on their hinges and didn't close properly. Work that would need to be done to put the place on the market.

Returning to Crossroads Creek was not without deeper problems. Emotionally, it left him in a dark place where he would have to fight his past demons. In his mind, he could see his sister playing, the pain of it catching him off guard. His father riding back to the house for lunch, tall on his majestic stallion, and in command of life, the man a stern taskmaster when it came to his son. His sweet mother in the garden picking flowers for the kitchen table, always greeting her husband with a ready smile. Unwelcome memories flooded his brain. The pain of knowing they died in a tragic car accident and weren't coming back suffocated him the same way it had twenty years ago.

And the accident had been all his fault.

His sleep had been tormented by nightmares last night, and he steeled himself for more of the same. If only he could turn back the hands of time and undo some of the decisions he'd made as a kid.

But life didn't give do-overs. And when Liam left at the end of the three weeks, he would sell the house. The devastating memories were far stronger than the happy ones.

Mandy couldn't believe it. The day had gone from bad to worse. Not only did she not get the promotion, but she would be saddled with an officer who needed babysitting. The new captain was still a rookie to her way of thinking. He hadn't spent years cultivating relationships and arresting hardened criminals or investigating cases.

Her fingers brushed her badge, a reminder of all she'd done and been through to get to this point in life, but she still lost out. More than a little frustrated, she wanted to quit. Start over. Somewhere other than a cowboy town intent on continuing the good ole' boys' club in the police department. It wouldn't hurt to put out feelers, but in the meantime, she wanted answers.

She made her way to the chief's office after the briefing, closing the door behind her with a little more force than necessary. Privacy was in order, even if anyone looking on could see what was happening. Everyone in the department knew the job was supposed to have been hers. Whether or not they agreed with the twist of events didn't matter. What they wouldn't like was a stranger in their midst, especially one who appeared to have been handed a promotion on a silver platter. *Literally.*

"Chief Jackson, I'd like to know what just happened in there?" Mandy asked, coming straight to the point.

"Have a seat, Sergeant Peters. And need I remind you I'm the boss here, so be careful what lines you cross when you question my judgement."

Mandy sat down and took a deep breath, inhaling the fresh coffee aroma and trying to use it as aromatherapy to help her calm down.

She wasn't looking to get fired and needed to recenter her thoughts. She touched her cross pendant, praying for the right words. "I'm well aware of your position here. I'm also well aware that I deserved that promotion, and you gave it to some rookie law enforcement officer that has more street time than anything else to recommend him for the job. What gives? I think I deserve an explanation."

The chief had the good grace to look remorseful, but it changed nothing. She kept quiet, waiting for him to explain.

"He's a good police officer. Perhaps not as experienced, but you can help him. His last boss and I are friends, and he highly recommended him. It's a favor of sorts. This sort of stuff happens all the time and you know it." The tapping of his pencil on the desk was most irritating, but she also knew it was one of the chief's tells. It meant he wasn't as happy with the change in personnel as one would expect. He just had no plans to explain his reasoning to her.

"That's nonsense. I earned that position."

"Sorry, Sergeant Peters. Honestly. My hands are tied on this." He rose and started to pace, as though he couldn't bear to look her straight in the face.

Mandy fumed. "Sounds to me like someone got paid off to make this happen."

The chief scowled, his forehead a ravine of wrinkles. "I resent that remark. Like I said, I'm sorry. You need to let this go."

She shook her head. "I can't. I'm thinking of leaving the department. Maybe it's time I went elsewhere. I'm tired of being passed over because I'm a woman."

"I wish you wouldn't do that, and this has nothing to do with you being a woman. I value everything you've done for CCPD. Let me talk to the town council and see if there's any room in the budget for two captains. I'll think of something. You deserve a promotion. I'm not challenging that aspect of the equation. Give me a few weeks to see what I can put together. In the meantime, help Captain Carter get settled in. It's a huge ask, I know. But I'm asking anyway."

Mandy sat back in her chair and crossed her legs. "I don't know. We both know CCPD can't afford two captains. My entire focus has been on my career. I'll ride with him because you've ordered me to, and I won't just up and quit without another job. You've got three weeks to figure something out. Let's just hope he doesn't get me killed."

The chief chuckled, a look of relief crossing his face. "It's not like he's fresh out of school."

"It doesn't matter. He's arrogant and clearly has connections. Not a good combo in my book. He better know how to follow directions, is all I'm saying." Mandy walked out of the chief's office and let out a deep breath. She hadn't been able to change a thing, least of all, to get out of working with the newbie.

Mandy: Cancel tonight.

Jenna: Why?

Mandy: No reason now. I didn't get the promotion. Some city-beat officer got it. And best of all, I get to babysit him. :/

Jenna: No way.

Mandy: Way.

Jenna: So sorry. I can't believe your boss led you to believe the position would be yours.

Mandy: Tell me about it. I told him I'm going to look elsewhere for a new job.

Jenna: You wouldn't actually leave, would you?

Mandy: I would. In fact, I'm going to put out some feelers. There's just one other blip in this disaster. I can't believe I was assigned to partner with this rookie for the next three weeks while the chief tries to figure something else out for me.

Jenna: Is he cute?

Mandy: I'm rolling my eyes and won't justify that question with an answer.

Jenna: Which means yes.

Mandy: I plead the fifth.

It was her big mouth that got her stuck riding with the guy. A mistake she wouldn't make again. But as she headed back to her desk, she couldn't help shake the feeling that God had a reason for all of this—she just wished He'd let her in on what it was.

Chapter Four

LIAM MADE HIS WAY to Sergeant Peters' desk. He had stalled talking to her as long as possible. He hoped the extra time to stew over the sudden change would help her accept the inevitable, swallow the bitter pill of defeat, and get back to her work. If she was as good a police officer as Chief Jackson indicated, it was certainly what Liam expected. "Ready to roll, Sergeant Peters?"

"Roll?" She rolled her eyes and shook her head to make a point. So much for swallowing the bitter pill. Apparently, it was still choking her. "We don't roll."

"Oh, small town lingo. *Hmmm*, let me guess—are we going for a ride along?" he teased, shooting her a wink.

"Neither," she scoffed, grabbing a set of keys off her desk and then heading down the hall without so much as another word. She didn't even attempt to be cordial.

"Then what?" he persisted, following closely. He'd play it her way for the time being. It suited his purpose for everyone to think he wasn't a threat and for his new partner to think she was in control.

She stopped and swung around to face him, hands on hips. "It's just two partners working a shift as we drive around Crossroads Creek, making sure nothing is going on. Occasionally, we hand out tickets, but mostly we follow up on leads after a crime is committed. It isn't a hot seat of activity, so I'm sure you'll be bored by the end of the day. Do you think you can handle that, *Captain Carter*?"

Liam grinned. The morning sunlight caught her badge as she stood there, defiant. One thing was for sure, work wouldn't be boring with Sergeant Peters around. "Of course. Lead the way, partner."

"First, we need to stop by the supply room and get uniforms. You don't look very official in a dress shirt, tie, and slacks. Just saying." She pushed open the door and pointed at the shelves of clothes. "I don't know your size, so I'll let you pick out what you need. You get three of everything. Change in the bathroom across the hall."

It had been quite a while since he had to wear a blue uniform, but it was all part of his cover. "Thirty-four neck, thirty-six sleeve, thirty-two waist, and thirty-six pant leg. Just in case you were curious." Liam grinned as he pulled the garments from the shelves, knowing full well Peters was ready to blow a fuse, but unable to resist teasing her.

"I'm not," she seethed.

Liam held up the clothes and started for the restroom.

"Pick a locker that doesn't have a lock for the extras."

"Yes, ma'am," Liam said, a hint of laughter tinging his remark so she wouldn't take offense. He stowed the extra uniforms and his street clothes in a locker. They were stiff and needed a good washing but he would deal with that tonight. Right now, his focus was on Sergeant Peters and trying to figure out a way to get along with his new prickly partner.

"You'll need to stop by Chief Jackson's office for your badge," she said with tightly controlled anger in her voice.

"Already taken care of," he said, pulling the badge from his pocket and pinning it in place. "Is it straight? Wouldn't want someone to think I was a rookie officer," he said, knowing it was exactly what Peters was thinking.

"It's fine. Can we go now?"

"Lead the way, Sergeant Peters."

She led him to the patrol car and Liam automatically made his way to the driver's side.

Peters beat him to it. "Not a chance. I'll drive. Maybe it will help you learn the area." She pulled open the door and slid inside, not bothering to wait for his response.

This wasn't a battle he wanted to fight anyway. "Of course. I should have thought of that." He knew the area all too well, but he wouldn't want to let on. Luckily, Peters seemed slightly placated by his easy acquiescence, as though begrudgingly forced to recognize he wasn't a total jerk.

She eased out of the parking lot onto Main Street. "Our job is to keep our eyes open and cruise the area. Tell me if you see anything happening that doesn't look right or warrants checking out. But first, today's itinerary includes a visit to the Fiskars' Farm on the outskirts of town. Mrs. Fiskar reported a missing pig this morning and believes it was stolen."

Surely Peters was pranking him as a first-day initiation. "Did Mrs. Fiskar check to see if Charlotte left a message in her web to help solve the crime?" he teased.

Peters shook her head. "Not everything is a joke around here, *Captain Carter.* I take my job seriously," she added, frowning over at him.

A glimmer in the sergeant's eyes betrayed her amusement, though she fought to suppress it. "Look, I know you're not happy that I'm here. Sometimes, life deals us lemons and we have to move on. Can we call a truce? We have to work together, and it would be great if we could enjoy the time, and you weren't carrying a grudge like a heavy stone around your neck and waiting to find fault with everything I say or do."

"You got my job. That's different." She huffed, not giving an inch.

Chief Jackson had mentioned she would react strongly. Liam would do his best to find a middle ground for them while he was in town. "Still, we need to work together. Can't we make the best of what you consider a bad situation? I'm quite happy with the promotion, and they must think I'm qualified. Perhaps you should give me the same benefit of the doubt, Sergeant Peters."

"Qualified? I highly doubt it, judging by what I've seen already. Make no mistake, *Captain Carter*, I will find out how you got the job. I don't believe for one minute that you earned the position," Peters said, sticking to her earlier stance on the subject.

There was only so much of the rookie police officer imagery he could play into without losing all credibility. "Since we're partners, I guess you'll get to find out firsthand. Give me a chance, and you might be surprised with the outcome." Pride pushed him to answer differently than he should. Liam shifted in his seat, conscious of how close to the truth his words actually landed. It wasn't as if he was actually saying anything wrong, just trying to set the record straight for when the truth came out.

"Not likely, Captain Carter. I'll be watching you every step of the way."

"I'm sure you will be," Liam added, keeping his voice non-committal and flat. Any good police officer would want to lock beneath the surface of his sudden arrival on the scene. Which is exactly why they made sure his background story was firmly in place and all documentation in order. He was Liam Carter for the next three weeks, and it was his job to make sure they never found his true identity.

They pulled up to the Fiskar farm and parked in front of the house. A portly woman met them on the porch, fanning her face, even though it was still early and not even remotely considered hot out yet. The July heat would come soon enough. July in Texas was always on the hot side of comfortable.

"Thank you for coming, Mandy. I told Edith when I talked to her on the phone that you had to be the one to come out and get the infor-mation. Guys don't understand how much we women can care about animals and I'm just so worried about what someone will do to Porky. She's such a sweet pig and part of the family. The grandkids will be so upset she's missing."

Mrs. Fiskar wiped at the tears that trickled down her face.

Peters patted the woman's arm. "You did right calling this in," she said, shooting Liam a look that dared him to contradict her. "Just tell me what you know, and I'll write up the report. Pigs are pets and we understand how upsetting it can be when something goes wrong. We'll do our best to find her. With any luck, she just ran off for an adventure and we can locate her this morning."

Mrs. Fiskar dabbed at her eyes with a tissue. "I hope you're right, dear. I fed her last night, and she was fine. When I went to feed her this morning, she was gone. That's all I know."

"Did you check the fence for holes she might have gotten out through?" Peters questioned.

Liam couldn't believe they were investigating the disappearance of a pig. Talk about a first.

"I checked and there's nothing big enough for a pig the size of Porky to escape through. And the fence gate is still latched. Porky didn't walk out of here on her own accord. She wouldn't because she loves me and loves the treats I give her," Mrs. Fiskar said, clutching one hand to her heart dramatically.

"Yes, she's a well-fed and well-loved pet and you've always done your best with her. Everyone knows that."

Liam had enough of this nonsense and was determined to put an end to it. He had played along, but only to expedite the entire process. "What about the barn door? Was it accidentally left open and perhaps Porky squeezed under the bottom of the fence?"

Both women turned to him, surprise on their faces, as though they had forgotten he was standing there.

"Who's this?" Mrs. Fiskar asked, pointing at him.

"The new police captain in Crossroads Creek," Mandy offered, her voice reflecting her disdain and leaving nothing to the imagination in figuring out how she felt about his arrival in town.

Mrs. Fiskar sized him up and nodded. "The barn door was open, but I close and latch it every night. And as for squeezing anywhere, it's doubtful considering her size. She won first place at the fair this year," she beamed with pride.

It would seem Liam had passed muster. As to motive, that was easy now that he had a clear picture of the animal in question. A porky pig would bring a good price at market. He kept that observation to himself, not wanting to upset the woman further. "Then it would seem your pig was stolen. Did you notice any odd lights last night? Or sounds?"

Mrs. Fiskar shook her head, her shoulders drooping further as she tried to face the reality. "No. Not a thing. I should have been more careful with a prized pig. Especially my beloved Porky," she added, her voice quivering with sadness.

"Anyone trying to get you to sell the pig to them recently? Or acting more interested than usual at the fair?" Liam asked.

Mrs. Fiskar's eyes opened wide, her chin rising a notch as though he'd struck a chord. "Come to think of it, Ronald Thompson did offer to buy her. He wasn't happy when I wouldn't sell her and said some mean things to me. Do you think he stole her?" she asked.

He didn't need her going down the rabbit hole chasing leads. *More like a piggy hole.* He suppressed a smile at his own mental correction, trying to find humor in the situation. "I don't know. Probably not. It s too obvious, but it'll be worth looking into," Liam said.

"Was Porky acting any different yesterday? Is there any chance she's hiding somewhere because she's not feeling well? You might have accidentally left the barn door open," Mandy added, not to be outdone by his line of questioning. It was a valid question and observation.

Mrs. Fiskar tapped her chin and thought about it for a few seconds. "I never leave the door open. And well, now that you mention it, Porky seemed a little off yesterday. Perhaps we could look around the barn and the farm a little better."

Liam frowned. He didn't relish walking around the farm in search of a missing pig. These were sights and sounds he'd left far behind twenty years ago—by choice.

"Absolutely, Mrs. Fiskar. Captain, why don't you check the barn, and we'll check the perimeter of the barn and house," Peters said, taking back control of the situation.

Without making them both look bad, he had little choice but to agree. Turnabout was fair play, and the next time around, he would have the upper hand. "That's fine." It was totally the opposite of what he wanted, but he wouldn't give her the satisfaction of knowing she had won the round.

Liam made his way to the barn, the familiar scent of hay and farm animals assailing him. A mare hung its head over the stall gate, watching him with interest. Without thinking, he walked over to the horse and patted the side of her neck. "Good girl. I'm Liam and I see your name is Lily." Pretty name for a pretty horse. The Bald Face markings on her face were like Fancy's markings, and a pang of nostalgia hit him. He loved his horse, but when Liam left, he didn't plan to return. Terrance had sold Fancy at his request.

Riding was the one thing he found solace in doing at a time in his life when being a kid wasn't easy. It was something he missed the most from his childhood, that and his dog Poncho. Expectations to be good, pressure to be bad. Knowing that only the strong survived. It was a balancing act for sure, and there were plenty of kids at school that loved to bully others. "One day, I'll have a beautiful mare again, just like you," Liam said, rubbing her forehead. Lily nudged his arm as if in approval and snorted. *Though if he stay in Dallas, it would never happen.*

He moved on, checking all the stalls for the horses, the sheep, and the empty one with the name Porky on the sign. An orange and white Tabby cat ran across his path, jumping up on the stall gate, meowing at him. Liam continued his search, looking everywhere he could think of that would hold a pig of such magnitude. The cat jumped down and ran to a bale of hay in the back corner of the barn, looking at him expectantly. "What is it, girl?" he asked, moving to pet the cat, wondering what she wanted.

Out of the corner of his eye, he spotted a curly tail moving behind the bale of hay. He ducked down and stuck his head through the opening to check the back wall, only to discover Porky. The pig looked up at him and laid her head back down. "What's a matter, Porky? You don't feel good by the looks of you," Liam said, not a novice with ranch animals. "Hang in there, and I'll get you some help."

He stood and turned, but his foot slid, and Liam came to a stop, the aroma of fresh manure permeating his brain. His lip curled in distaste as he looked down and discovered he'd stepped into a pile of pig manure. He tried to use the straw to remove some of the offending substance, but it was only making it worse, the stench assailing him and causing him to pull back.

So much for clean shoes and making an impression on people. Though it occurred to him, it was the perfect way to get back at Mandy. She wouldn't appreciate the manure odor in her clean patrol car. Liam chuckled to himself.

It was perfect.

Chapter Five

♥

CAPTAIN CARTER'S LINE OF questions to Mrs. Fiskar had been fired off with a level of expertise Mandy hadn't expected. Not to be outdone, she opened up a different avenue of plausibility. One that ended in a search in which the captain turned up one sick pig hiding in a corner behind a crate in the barn. Dr. Granger was called, and luckily, Porky would be okay. A case of indigestion was rare, but then it would seem the sweet treats Mrs. Fiskar was feeding the pig weren't the best choice, according to the local vet.

It all worked out, except for the reservations Mandy had about Captain Carter. From rookie to sergeant to captain in a couple of years. It certainly raised a few questions and a few eyebrows of the other officers, including her. Tonight, she planned to do a little more digging on the captain after he left the station. Not that she could ferret out much without a court order or subpoena, but she would find out everything she could based on available public records.

What should have been a night to celebrate would become a night to investigate her new temporary partner. Something didn't look or feel right about the guy. Good-looking didn't mean he wasn't without backing or deep pockets orchestrating his successful career promotion. Dirty cop? Maybe, but doubtful. She considered herself an excellent judge of character, and the only thing she had against him was a stolen promotion.

So far.

They needed to head back to the station to fill out the reports and close the case of the missing pig. "Let's go, Captain," she said, making her way back to the patrol car without waiting for him to answer. She slid in the car, but when he joined her, a terrible odor permeated the entire vehicle. "What's that smell?" she asked, scrunching her nose as the odor grew stronger with each passing second.

Captain Carter turned to face her, a grin on his face that spelled trouble. "Pig manure. That's what happens when you search a barn. Sorry."

Except his smile only widened, contradicting his attempt to make her believe he was truly sorry. More than likely, he was enjoying her discomfort and her reaction. "Well then, seeing as you're the new guy, guess you can clean the patrol car when we get back to the office," Mandy said, doing her best to hold her own against the overly confident lawman. She'd noticed the strong odor but only thought it was the farm itself, not her partner.

"You're forgetting one thing," he said, casting her a glance, one eyebrow raised.

"What's that?" she asked, frowning.

"I'm the captain. Your boss. So, I guess you have cleaning duty," he added, entirely too satisfied with himself.

A flash of frustration surged through her. Mandy wanted to scream, but she wouldn't give him the satisfaction. "Fine," she ground out. There was no way she would let him win this battle of wills. Men always thought she would be easy to push around, but she'd show him differently.

"Or we could do it together. It's only fair. You were the one who made me search the barn. Though I was supposed to be looking for a pig, not pig manure." He chuckled.

Whether she wanted it to or not, her respect for him rose a notch. He didn't have to suggest a compromise, seeing as he was, in fact, the boss. It would seem the new captain was full of surprises. "Thanks. I'll take you up on the offer."

"What's on the agenda next, Sergeant Peters?" he asked, his eyes watering a bit.

"Oh, for heaven's sake, enough with the Sergeant Peters. Call me Mandy unless it's official business, since we will be spending lots of time together." He had after all found the pig and saved the day. That in itself should warrant a first name basis.

"Thank you, Mandy. And you can call me Liam. Does that mean we're friends?"

"Hardly. Work partners as in my backup."

"I think it's the other way around and you're my backup." Liam shot her a wink.

It was true, but she didn't have to like it. "To answer your earlier question, we need to go back and fill out our report. If you can see through your tears, that is." Mandy couldn't help but tease him, the opening was just too good.

"The smell is stronger on my side. Trust me. Why don't we swing by where I'm staying and hose off the floor mat and my shoes? It won't take us long and it's got to be better than riding around with my, *umm*, aroma." He grinned.

Mandy nodded, all too eager to get away from the odor before it clung to her skin and hair. The guys back in the office would have a field day over this if they found out. "Sounds good to me. Where are you staying?" She was more than a little curious about this man who landed in town and landed her job.

"2010 Lineberry Road," Liam replied, without hesitation.

"I heard the Whitakers moved to Colorado, but wasn't aware anyone new rented the old Calhoun ranch." Mandy prided herself on knowing everything going on in town. People came and left, but not so often you didn't take notice.

"I only arrived in town yesterday. I'm not settled in yet, but I'll make do for the time being."

"Will you eventually buy a place in Crossroads Creek? There's not much for sale in the area but you can check with Paul at Mayberry Realty. Homesteads don't change hands much," she offered, more for the purposes of doing some fact checking on him the easy way...by asking.

Liam seemed to contemplate his answer for a couple of seconds longer than she would have expected. Keen observation was imperative in her line of work, though perhaps he simply didn't know yet. The decision to buy or rent was always a big one, but Mandy was glad she bought a place of her own a couple of years ago. A small cottage with a decent-sized front and back yard was more than she needed to enjoy the peace when she wasn't working.

"I'm not sure what I'm doing. The place I'm staying needs fixing up so I might tackle a few things while I'm there. I'm in no rush to do much else."

Mandy frowned. "Why don't you have the caretaker of the ranch fix what's needed? Terrance McCallister has managed the place for almost twenty years and I'm sure he'd take care of anything you've noticed. Surely you'll have your hands full getting settled in and learning the area."

"He's out of town for a couple of weeks, and honestly, I don't mind. It's always good to focus on more than just work and projects give me a sense of satisfaction when completed. As a kid, I used to tinker with things, though inevitably most stuff turned out to be disastrous. I was hardheaded and didn't follow instructions well," he said, his voice taking on a tone of regret. "Luckily, I'm handier now than I was as a boy."

Interesting. "So where did you grow up?" she asked, trying to glean information that would help her understand Liam.

"I'm sure you'll figure that out tonight when you pull a background check on me." Liam grinned.

Mandy arched one eyebrow up, feigning shock. "What makes you think I plan on doing that?"

"The chief holds you in high regard. I would expect nothing less than a thorough research of my life."

Mandy chuckled. "Fair enough. Too bad I need a warrant for the really important stuff I might find. So, tell me something I won't get from the report. Why Crossroads Creek? Seems a far cry from the city, and you obviously told someone you wanted to be transferred here. Is there a woman involved? Perhaps you're in love?"

"Nothing could be further from the truth. I don't do relationships. The city is a hustle and bustle all the time. Guess I just want an easier job. You know, ride around the country all day and get paid for it." Liam winked, his grin all too devastatingly handsome. And irritating.

And just like that, they were right back where they started. Mandy wasn't buying his lackadaisical attitude.

She pulled down the driveway and headed for the side of the house where Liam pointed. The spigot was easy to spot, and she pulled close, making sure a hose would reach.

Liam hopped out of the car, glanced around, then frowned.

"What's wrong?" she asked.

"There's no hose hanging on the bracket. I'll need to go get one." Liam headed for the barn, Mandy following. He held the door open for her and then made his way toward the back. He reached for the green garden hose lying on the ground and coiled it up. "Grab the sprayer. It should be over there in the tool box," he said, pointing to the red metal unit in the corner on the work table.

Mandy pulled open the first drawer on the right. It was filled with sockets and drill attachments. She tried the next drawer and found an assortment of nuts and bolts. With at least ten more drawers to check, there was no telling what else she would find.

"Try the third one down on the left," Liam said, sliding the now coiled hose over his shoulder.

Mandy was more than a little surprised with his exact directive, and even more surprised the sprayer was right where he had told her to look. "How did you know that?" she asked, turning to face him as she held up the sprayer.

"Good guess based on the size of the drawer and the size of a sprayer," he teased.

"Not likely."

Liam shrugged. "I was out here yesterday poking around. What's the big deal?"

There wasn't one. Except she was trying to make more of Liam's sudden appearance and was perhaps reading more into everything he said or did. "Oh. That works."

"Speaking of work, let's get to this. I can't handle the smell much longer. It seems to stay with me." Liam chuckled.

"You can clean your shoes. Use a stick to get the crud out of the cracks and grooves. I'll deal with the floor mat," Mandy said, grimacing as he came close.

"So, you get the easy job?" he asked, as they headed back to the car.

"They are your shoes. And if I clean them, they are more than likely going to end up soaking wet. It's your choice, Captain Carter." She tried to keep the laughter out of her voice. Not that she would do it intentionally, though the thought of spraying Liam crossed her mind.

He nodded. "Point taken given you hate me right now."

"I don't hate you. I just don't understand why you got my job." There was no sense in avoiding the elephant that stood between them.

"I'm sorry," he offered. It looked as though he would like to say more but began hooking up the hose instead.

Mandy believed him. It didn't change the fact that his sudden appearance was out of the ordinary, or that it was only right she tried to figure out why it happened. Even if the chief wasn't willing to tell her what really happened.

Chapter Six

♥

OVER THE WEEK, LIAM and Mandy fell into a routine pattern. Briefing first thing in the morning, then riding patrol the rest of the day, with scattered meal breaks. Slowly, but surely, they were getting to know each other. Little things, like that Mandy preferred black coffee. Old-fashioned donuts were her favorite, but every now and then, she'd treat herself to a chocolate-covered donut. That was always fun because inevitably, she would end up with icing on her chin or cheek, and he never missed the opportunity to tease her. They both loved Chicken Caesar salad on a spinach wrap as a fairly healthy option for lunches, the opposite of their hankering for pizza. And of course the occasional hot dog from Hot Dogs Are Us. Those ranked as his favorite hot dogs ever. They liked different toppings, but neither one ever said no to eating in the park.

Liam also figured out she didn't talk about her private life. And from what he could tell, she lived for her job and did little else...the same work principle he possessed. Young, beautiful, and professional, but withdrawn from the real world. It didn't add up and Liam wanted to know more. His past dictated who he was, but what was Mandy's story?

Whenever he could, Liam visited businesses, talked to people on the street, and stopped in at the local eateries. The Golden Spoon had great breakfast options, but the diner was also a great source of people watching, listening, and asking questions. Nothing specific, but always with a purpose to get them talking. The same was true for Fontana and Wylie, though unless he wanted to gain ten pounds in the time he was here, he limited himself to coffee and an occasional dessert pastry. The bakery in Fontana was heavenly and one day, he'd like to take Mandy with him, but it would risk her asking too many questions. Squeezing in those times when Mandy wasn't around was always more difficult and limited.

Mandy would make an excellent detective, and he'd put in a good word for her when he returned to Dallas. It wasn't just her keen sense of observation, but also her ability to talk to people. Get them to give her information in a roundabout way so they didn't realize they were being interrogated. Granted, the local cases didn't amount to much more than an occasional break-in or a missing animal, but he had a feeling she could apply herself in any situation.

Luckily, the other officers in the CCPD didn't seem to mind him anymore, having resigned themselves to the fact he was the new captain. Every chance Liam got, he saw them in action, looking for some sort of clue. A lead. But so far, nothing had turned up, no warning bells going off in his head.

After checking in with Chief Wilcox back in Dallas, Liam realized it was time to put more focus on some of the other neighboring towns. The trick was to get an opening to meet the officers and casually observe them.

Mandy returned from the ladies' room and slid into the booth across from him. They had caught a late breakfast at the diner to avoid the morning rush.

"Anything special on our agenda today?" Mandy asked.

"Well, there wasn't anything assigned to us, because the woman from last night's domestic abuse call refused to file charges. But I'd like us to stop by and check on her. More specifically, have *you* talk to her. *Woman to woman.* Get her to understand that we can protect her, but she's got to trust us. If anyone can get her to see reason, it would be you," Liam said.

Mandy smiled, a genuine heart-warming smile that made his heart do flip-flops. "That's a high compliment, Captain Carter."

When she wasn't trying to figure him out and trip him up, they got along amazingly well. This was one of those times. "You deserve it."

"Based on?" she asked.

Liam returned her smile. "Observation. It doesn't take a rocket scientist to see how good you are with people. You connect in ways that folks feel your genuine care and concern."

Mandy blushed, her cheeks a pretty shade of pink. "Thank you. You're not so bad yourself, though I won't admit it to anyone else," she teased, shooting him a wink.

"Why is that?"

Mandy leaned back, arms crossed over her chest, pausing before she answered. "Honestly, I don't want to like you. Apart from the fact I find you edgy and dedicated to the job, I can't figure you out. Or find anything wrong with you. Initially, you seem to have a...for the lack of a better word, lackadaisical attitude. But seeing you in action, you're anything but.

So why the subterfuge?" She leveled him with her bright blue eyes as they locked with his.

"Call it first day nerves." His stomach clenched at the half-truth. He would give anything to tell her the truth, but she had reasoned out on her own he wasn't a rookie. What she did with that knowledge had yet to be seen.

"Doubtful, but I'll—" Mandy's gaze suddenly sharpened, her attention riveted on an unhappy young girl, perhaps ten or eleven years old, standing next to their booth toward the front of the diner. Uncombed mousy brown hair hung down the girl's back in long tresses.

The girl stomped her foot. "I want my mom."

"Sit down," the woman scolded. "You're making a scene," she said, reaching for the child.

The girl turned and flounced out of the restaurant, disregarding the woman's directive entirely. Mandy was on her feet in a split second and followed the girl outside. Liam was on his feet and headed for the woman still sitting in the booth.

"Pardon me, ma'am. Is everything okay?"

The woman nodded. "Everything is fine. I'm just trying to have breakfast and I ain't bothering no one. I would appreciate it if you would mind your own business," she huffed.

Liam tapped his badge. The woman's worn-out shirt and jeans, and her scruffy sneakers were similar to what the girl had on. "It's my job to check things out when something seems wrong, or at least questionable. So, is that your daughter?" he asked, pointing to the girl talking outside with Mandy.

The woman frowned. "Hardly. She's my niece. I'm sick and tired of covering for my sister. I have a life of my own and it's not taking care of her brat when she's too tired to do it herself."

"What's wrong with your sister?"

"She likes to go out and have fun until the wee hours of the night."

Liam relaxed. It was an unfortunate situation, but one that didn't elicit intervention. However, with the recent kidnapping, it would pay to go the extra mile. "Perhaps I can talk to your sister for you. What's her name and where can I find her?"

The woman's eyes narrowed to thin slits. "She's at the place we rented last night, and that won't be necessary. We are just passing through town on our way to Dallas," the woman snarled. "Unless I've committed some crime, I would like you to leave me alone—Captain Carter," she added as she squinted to read his badge and name tag, then returned to stare him down.

"No crime, but just a warning. Your niece shouldn't be left alone outside. We've had a recent kidnapping near here and I'm sure you wouldn't want anything to happen to her." He paid close attention to her reaction, but it would seem her only crime was a lack of warmth and heart for her niece. But he would check out her story. *Just in case.*

"Oh, I hadn't heard. Reckon I should get our breakfast and get back to my sister. Girl can go without food if she don't want to eat." She huffed as she grabbed her purse and hoisted herself out of the booth and headed for the register.

Liam followed. "What did you say your name was?"

"I didn't, but it's Patty Whitaker. And my sister is Tracy Whitaker. Check it out. Talk to her. I don't care. We haven't done any-thing to break the law, and I'm tired of you hassling me." She turned to the server. "Can you make my order to-go? My *niece* is caus-ing trouble," she added, glaring up at Liam.

Christina nodded. "No problem. I'll let them know in the back and have it ready for you shortly." The server didn't blink an eye or crack a smile, but then perhaps she had already had a run-in with the surly woman.

"If you don't mind, *Captain Carter*, I'll go grab my niece. Who knows what tales she's spinning to your partner while you keep me talking in here?"

Liam's warning bells went off, though he still had nothing to go on. "Just one thing before you go. Any chance you have some ID?" At the very least, he was buying Mandy some time to talk to the girl, if for no other reason than to reassure them she was okay.

"Of all the—" the woman ground out, the rest of her sentence left unsaid as she dug through her purse. She shoved her driver's license in his face and Liam noted the name and face were a match for the woman standing in front of him, and that she was from Albuquerque, New Mexico.

At least she hadn't lied about her identity. "You're good to go. Thanks."

"Here's your order and your check," Christina said, handing both to the woman. Her smile faded as Patty snatched them out of her hand.

She reviewed the bill and handed Christina a twenty and then waited for her change. Without leaving a tip, Patty turned and stormed off, leaving Liam to watch and wonder.

He slid a five across the counter. "Thanks."

"Thank you, Captain." Her smile blossomed with genuine gratitude.

A knot of unease settled in his stomach. They would definitely check out the motel and the woman's story. But first, he wanted to compare notes with Mandy and find out about her discussion with the young girl. Ms. Whitaker rushed to her niece's side and grabbed her hand. She exchanged words with Mandy and then took off down the street, tugging the girl behind.

Mandy couldn't believe the nerve of Kendra's aunt. The child verified the woman in the restaurant was, in fact, her aunt. And that nothing was amiss. Was it the truth or a cover story made up out of fear? There was no way to know for sure, but she hoped the young girl was telling the truth. Either that or she was an excellent actress.

She headed back inside, spotting Liam at the register. Mandy moved to join him, curious why the change of plans. "What's going on? Aren't we eating breakfast?"

Liam shrugged. "We are, but not here. Christina is bagging up our order for us to take with us. I caught the gist of what was happening at the same time you bolted out of the diner and while you were out there talking to the girl, I was questioning the aunt in here."

The man was full of surprises. Good ones. "Nice work, partner."

"Thanks. The woman's name is Patty Whitaker and she and her sister, Tracy, are on their way to Dallas with the girl, or so she claims. I figure we should check out Patty's story and eat on the way."

Proactive was always a plus in her books and she liked the fact that Liam had the same quality. It would seem they had a lot in common, though she never would have expected it when they first met. "Sounds good. So where are we headed?" Mandy asked.

"To the place she's staying in town. Which would mean the B&B. Patty seems upset with Tracy because she stays out and parties all night, though I don't gather either comes across as mother material. Her sister is tired of being dumped on with watching the girl," Liam's voice held a note of concern that echoed through the patrol car's interior.

"Janice Edwins, the owner will tell us anything we want to know."

"Good. That makes it quicker."

Mandy nodded. "The girl's name is Kendra, and she said pretty much the same thing. I wonder what the mother is up to, that she's not available to watch her daughter?"

"That's what we need to find out. Considering the recent kidnapping in Wylie, we can't help but check into the situation." Liam put the car into drive and headed for the B&B.

Mandy shuddered, the word alone enough to make her feel ill as she recalled her situation.

"You don't think they ki...n...napped Kendra, do you? It wouldn't fit the case profile," she said, swallowing hard as she tamped down the revulsion growing in the pit of her stomach. A prayer silently formed in her head, a habit born of years of struggle. Oh, how she hated that word.

"Do you know much about the Wylie kidnapping case two months ago? I'd think the CCPD was called in to help search, and you'd be privy to the details."

Mandy pulled back, trying to regroup and find the right words. "Just that a toddler around two years old was taken in the middle of the night. The father was away on a verified business trip and the mother must have forgotten to lock up. No signs of forced entry. And yes, we all helped search. There just wasn't much to go on. There never is." Her head was spinning, and she felt ill. Memories threatened to overwhelm her, a familiar battle she'd fought countless times before. It was always this way when she couldn't avoid the subject.

"I should request the case file from their chief of police, seeing as this happened just one town over." His fingers tightened on the steering wheel, turning them white. "Doing my due diligence as the new captain in the area." Not that he didn't already have them, but it kept the conversation moving forward.

"You could, but out here in the country, folks don't take too kindly to other folks checking behind them to make sure they did their job right. Especially law enforcement officers."

"I didn't say that's what I was doing. Only that I should familiarize myself with the case, and if they share the information, there's no harm done."

"Fine, you do that. Now, can we focus on Kendra, her mom, and her aunt? I hate talking about the kidnapping, if it's all the same to you." She tried to keep her tone flat and non-committal. Mandy had eight years of self-recrimination that she didn't do enough to protect her baby. She never stopped following the cases over the years, hoping something would lead her to discover what happened that dreadful night, but talking about them was another thing entirely. Talking opened up wounds for others to see, and she preferred to keep her private life...private. Otherwise, there were always too many questions...and suspicions.

The silence between them grew heavy, each lost in their own thoughts. She glanced over at Liam, wondering if he sensed the turmoil just beneath her carefully constructed exterior.

"Sometimes the worst cases are the ones that stay with you," Liam said softly, his voice carrying a weight of understanding that surprised Mandy. "The ones that haunt you long after the file has been closed or deemed unsolved with no leads and moved to the back-burner."

Mandy tensed, caught between wanting to shut down the conversation and feeling an unexpected connection to her new partner.

"You sound like you know something about that," she said, her words more an observation than an inquiry.

Liam's hands gripped the steering wheel a little tighter, his knuckles a bloodless white. "I do."

Mandy nodded, understanding more than she wanted to admit, realizing that perhaps Captain Carter also had his share of pain in the past.

Chapter Seven

MANDY'S TENSE, GUARDED REACTION when he started asking questions about the kidnapping case set off warning flags in Liam's head. What should have been a routine conversation about a recent kidnapping case that was headline news, turned into a case of evasion on her end.

The question was, why? It was the first time he sensed something was wrong with the otherwise by-the-book efficient officer he knew. Liam respected how hard she had worked to get where she was now in law enforcement, especially given she was a lot like him in that way. And he had been more than ready to remove her from the suspect list, but now he wasn't so sure of his decision. Doubt gnawed at the edges of his professional judgement, conflicting with his own internal radar about her character. Something he didn't like. After getting past her hard exterior, he had discovered her humor, work ethic, and the depth of her caring for others. Each layer showed a woman of remarkable resilience. Not to mention she possessed a wealth of information on all things Crossroads Creek.

Not that he needed it, but still good for the updates.

They arrived at the B&B, a well-kept large Victorian home with a wraparound porch that spoke of small-town hospitality and southern charm. He didn't see any cars with out-of-state tags, specifically New Mexico.

"I'll go talk to Janice Edwin and find out what room they're in," Mandy offered, sliding out of the car before he even shut the car off. "Be right back," she called, the door slamming shut behind her.

"Sure thing," Liam said, knowing full well she couldn't hear him. He pulled out his phone and typed a text to Chief Wilcox.

Liam: I'd like the HR file on Sergeant Mandy Peters. Can you send the authorization to Chief Jackson? There's something odd about her reaction when I brought up the kidnapping case and I'd like to have a look.

Chief Wilcox: Will do.

Liam: I've requested the HR file on Sergeant Peters. My boss will get you the authorization needed shortly.

Chief Jackson: Why?

Liam: Something came up today, and I'd like to look into her files.

He didn't feel the need to explain himself, preferring to keep his suspicions under wraps.

Chief Jackson: I don't like it. I would bet my career on her integrity.

Liam had to agree, but he still had a job to do. Years of detective work with the Texas

Rangers taught him to follow every lead, no matter how small or bullet proof. Not to mention, any oddity or possible lead was more than he had this morning when he woke up.

Liam: I hear you, but it's my job to leave no stone unturned. In fact, please send me the personnel files on all the employees. I should do the same for the Wylie and Fontana PD offices.

Chief Jackson: I won't stand in the way of an investigation, but I don't have to agree. You'll have them by this evening.

Liam: Thanks. I'll make sure you get the proper authorizations.

He clicked the off button once to darken his screen as Mandy came back to the car.

"There's no one by that name staying at the B&B. Maybe the woman meant the motel in Fontana? It's close to here," Mandy said, sliding back into the car.

It had been a mistake on his part not to ask the woman the name of the place, but he figured she meant here in town. Most people didn't drive fifteen miles away to get breakfast. He was sure the slipup hadn't gone unnoticed by Sergeant Peters. "Perhaps. We can drive over there and ask questions."

Mandy shook her head. "It's out of our jurisdiction."

Something Liam knew...except his jurisdiction covered a lot more territory. More like the entire state of Texas. "Of course, but it can't hurt to ask a couple of questions, right?" He was determined to follow up and make sure Kendra was okay.

"You're the boss." Mandy didn't like his decision, but she couldn't challenge it.

On the ride over, the silence between them was like a brick wall. And the best way he knew to break it down was to confront the issue. "Why don't you like discussing the kidnapping cases?"

Mandy sucked in a deep breath, visibly jerking back. "Why do you care?" she asked, her voice strained and slightly higher pitched than before.

"Professional interest, of course. You're a police officer and it's a case. Just strikes me as odd that you don't want to talk about it."

She twisted her fingers together, over and over, her silence deafening.

He waited.

Mandy turned to look out the window, keeping her face from his view. "Not everything is black and white," she ground out.

"What gives?"

Body language was key, and Mandy was showing some extremes. She pinned herself tight against the doorframe, as far from him as she could get. Her jaw was tightly clenched, and Liam could swear he heard her teeth grinding.

"You should have read my personnel file. Then you would already know I had a daughter. Now she's gone. The thought of parents losing children breaks my heart and it makes it hard to put one foot in front of the other. It's personal to me and I understand the parent's pain. So, can we drop it now?"

Liam was more than a little shocked at her admission. "I'm sorry. I didn't realize you were married, or that you had a child. I feel like a jerk for pressing you on this subject." He was at a loss for words. At least for the moment. He was all too familiar with the never-ending ache that went with losing people you loved.

"I'm not married. It's called divorced." Her voice quivered as she brushed back tears rolling down her face.

Liam wouldn't draw attention to them. Compassion softened his heart, and it occurred to him it was only right to share something of *his* personal life. He would share the pain of his past to close the gap between them and put them on the same foothold again. He never talked about his feelings with anyone, having buried them shortly after the accident that claimed the lives of his family. "I understand the pain of loss all too well. For me, it was my parents and my sister. They died in a car accident when a drunk driver struck their vehicle broadside, and it careened out of control over a cliff. Shortly after that, my girlfriend dumped me. It's like misery compounded by more misery. So yes, I understand, and I'm sorry for what you've been through and for making you think about it all over again."

Mandy slowly turned to face him, a question in her eyes. "Thank you. But what did you do to get past it all?"

Liam shook his head. "I didn't. It's not something I can ever move past because I feel guilty about what happened. That will never leave me. I just try not to think about it, which is why I'm sorry I made you do the same."

"I rest my case." Mandy smiled, though it was more like a quarter smile, the corners of her lips barely lifting upward. But it was enough to know she'd forgiven him. As though they were back on the same team. "I'm sorry for your loss," she added, reaching out to touch his arm.

A tenderness he hadn't felt in almost twenty years came over him. "Thank you. And yes, I got your point. You should have been an attorney," he added, hoping to change the subject and move into a less emotional topic.

"Funny enough, I started out for that role. To be an attorney, that is. Then everything changed after my divorce, and I went to the police academy instead."

It was a pretty big shift from law and order in a courtroom to law and order in the streets. "Do you regret it?"

Mandy shook her head. "Not at all. It keeps me busy. Some say I'm a workaholic, but it is what it is."

"Where did you go to the academy?" Liam asked.

"Austin. Eventually I transferred here to the CCPD."

Liam sucked in a deep breath. Subtle tension rippled down his spine. *Austin.* The city where the first kidnappings they had linked occurred. Cases tied based on patterns of how the crimes were committed "Do you like it here?" he asked, his brain racing in overload as he tried to digest this new information. He was never fond of coincidence.

"I love it here. Or at least I did until some city cop came in and stole my job." Mandy grinned.

"Touche." Liam pulled up to the Blue Cactus Motel and scanned the parking lot. No out-of-state tags on the vehicles. "I'll go do the questioning, so it's my job on the line and not yours."

"I like the sound of that." Mandy laughed.

The building was old and sat on the outskirts of town. Weathered blue paint and sagging structures that needed a massive facelift...or a teardown to start over. Judging by the looks of mostly bare railings, missing siding, roof patches and tarps, he couldn't imagine what the rooms looked like inside. This was one of those places where you judged a book by the cover and passed without stopping, leaving him to wonder why the inspectors had nothing to say about the place.

Five minutes later, he was back in the car. "The woman seems to have been telling the truth, though we just missed them. They checked out moments ago."

"What do you want to do about it?" Mandy asked.

Liam shrugged. Uncertainty was not a feeling he was comfortable with. But they had nothing to go on that would allow them to continue pursuing the Whitaker sisters. "What does your gut tell you about Kendra when you spoke to her?"

"That she was telling the truth. I didn't sense fear. She was mostly angry at leaving her friends to move to Dallas."

"Okay then. So that's how we play this out. I trust your instincts." Liam realized it was true. He also knew that in talking to Mandy, he was trying too hard to come up with a link and looking in innocent places. Just because her daughter died, and she was divorced, didn't make her a corrupt police officer or a criminal.

It made her a woman with heartache. A condition he was all too familiar with.

"Thank you. Your trust in my instinct means a lot to me," Mandy said.

"You're welcome." Liam put the car in gear and headed back toward town.

"If you don't mind me asking, why did your girlfriend leave you? And you don't have to answer. I'm just curious because you seem like a pretty good guy, much as I hate to admit it," Mandy added.

Having closed the subject, he was loath to let it resurface. But then he was the one who started the conversation down the dark path. "We were only seventeen, so it's not as traumatic as it sounds. Kids playing grownups in life. When she heard that folks in town blamed me for what happened to my family, she couldn't take the disgrace and dumped me. I even had a ring and was going to ask her to marry me."

Mandy frowned. "But why would they blame you? That sounds harsh."

"It was based on truth. Their disdain for me was nothing more than I deserved," Liam admitted, before he could stop from spilling his guts to his partner.

"Do you want to talk about it?"

Liam shook his head. "Not really. What's done is done. What about you? Why did you and your husband get a divorce?" It would be better to learn more about Mandy by asking questions than reviewing a file, and he was genuinely interested.

"Oddly enough, you and I are way too similar in that respect," Mandy said, her voice dropping a notch or two. Enough that he could barely hear her.

"What do you mean?"

The distant look in her eyes was as though she was lost in the misery of her past. "My husband left me because he blamed me the night we lost our daughter. Said I should have checked on her more often or paid more attention to the monitor. John got back late that night from a business trip and he was devastated. The police agreed with John, so I totally understand people wanting to place blame. Perhaps it makes it easier for them to accept whatever happened. I was never charged because there wasn't enough evidence that I was negligent, but it didn't stop people from talking. My ex made sure of that."

Liam was shocked to the core. "Unbelievable. The law says you're innocent until proven guilty. Your husband must have been a real jerk to turn against you that way."

Mandy nodded. "In his eyes, I was guilty from the start and that I wasn't a good mother. He married someone else not long after we divorced, and to add insult, I found out they had a daughter together. I figured he was having an affair as quickly as he moved on and started a new family."

That she was sharing such a deep emotional part of her past wasn't lost on Liam. "You're a lucky woman in that respect."

"What do you mean?" she asked, one eyebrow raised like he was crazy.

He patted her arm. "You're lucky to have lost such a loser."

"True. I just wish I had my daughter back," Mandy said, her voice catching on the last word.

"If you ever want to talk more about it, I can be a good listener. At least we both understand the devastating heartache and the inability to completely let go of the past," Liam said. And it had nothing to do with work. The bond they shared drew them closer together than he could have imagined, and he wanted to help her heal. Even if his own healing would never happen.

"Thanks. Truly. And it's a two-way street, you know."

Liam glanced at her. "I know it's a two-way street, but healing isn't something I'm ready to explore. I'm more of a one-way person."

Chapter Eight

❤

FOR THE PAST TWO days, neither she nor Liam broached the deep discussion they had previously, which was fine with Mandy. The unspoken understanding between them felt like a fragile truce. They were like two friends bonding together on the same side of an ugly fence. Her faith had seen her through the darkest days and still kept her making the best of life the only way she knew how. Liam seemed lost in his own past. Mandy couldn't imagine weathering the pain of such a crushing blow without God by her side.

"Another quiet day. Just the way I like it," Mandy said, smiling over at Liam as he drove down Main Street.

"I don't know. The slow pace is taking some getting used to. I'm almost wishing we had another lost pig call just for some action. Not that I want the pig to be sick, mind you." Liam grinned, clarifying what he meant.

Something he didn't have to do because she was certain he was one of the good guys in this world. "Of course not. But I, for one, can do without the odorific aromas you opted to bring into the patrol car last time. I swear I still get a whiff of pig manure. Not to mention, I'm pretty sure you enjoyed my reaction."

His grin widened, affirming her comment held more than a little truth. "It's your imagination."

Mandy rolled her eyes. Not that he could see. "Whatever. Hey, look. There's a sizable crowd gathered over there." She pointed toward the town's center park. Curiosity sparked her interest. "Want to check it out?"

"Absolutely." Liam parked down the street. They locked the car and headed toward the large gathering of people. "I don't remember anything posted for events on the bulletin board," he said, scanning the entire area.

"Me either. Hey, Betina. Are you taking a break from the Five & Dime to enjoy a lovely day at the park?" Mandy called out to the older woman off to the right.

She looked up and smiled, her gray hair and weathered wrinkly skin a testament to her age. "It is indeed. The sun is shining, and God is good. What more could we ask for?" Her eyes twinkled with the wisdom of her years. She was one of the most upbeat ladies at the church and always brightened a room.

"So true. What's going on here?" Mandy asked.

"Oh, such joy," Betina exclaimed. "The Turners were blessed with a litter of puppies and they're finally old enough to give away. Right cute if you ask me, but then, who doesn't love puppies? See for yourself," she said, walking back toward the throng of people.

"All this commotion for puppies?" Liam shook his head in disbelief.

"Puppies are adorable, and people love adorable anything. Babies, kittens, and puppies included. Come on, let's look. Can't hurt to see what all the fuss is about," Mandy said, following Betina.

They made their way to the front of the crowd, where several people were holding small gold and white long-haired puppies like babies and going gaga over them.

"Jenna, what are you doing here?" Mandy asked, spotting her friend as the crowd parted.

"I couldn't resist when I heard Max Turner would be here today, and that they were finally going to give their pups away. Isn't this the sweetest face ever? They are Border Collie Golden Retriever Mix puppies," Jenna turned the puppy she was holding to face Mandy.

The puppy's soft brown eyes seemed to plead for attention. She reached up and petted the dog. "I agree. I love the floppy ears and soft fur," Mandy said, enjoying the little rascal.

"You know, you could use a dog to keep you company. Here," Jenna said, holding the dog out for Mandy to take.

She shook her head. Owning a pet was a tremendous responsibility and not one she wanted. It would require her to open her heart to love again, something she swore she wouldn't do. A wall of protection welled up inside her.

"Come on. Are you afraid you'll fall in love?"

Exactly. Jenna knew her all too well. "Hardly," she said, and unable to resist the challenge, Mandy accepted the bundle of energy and held her close. The fresh scent of a clean puppy assailed her. "It's just a dog, and you know I don't have time to care for one." The puppy instantly laid its head against her chest and looked up. Their gazes caught. Soulful brown eyes that smiled as if only for her. She wouldn't fall for the puppy look. Mandy started to hand the puppy back, but it whined. A sound so pitiful, it pierced her carefully constructed defenses. She cradled the puppy closer and stroked its neck. The whining stopped.

"Looks like you have a new puppy," Liam teased, reaching out to rub the dog's ears and neck.

"Hardly. Why don't you take her? Being new in town, it might be nice for you to have a friend," she teased, hoping against hope he would take her up on the suggestion, if only so that the puppy had a home. *And not with her.*

"I think this little girl is already taken. She loves you." Liam laughed.

Mandy shook her head. "I don't know the first thing about puppies and—"

"Quit making excuses and adopt the puppy," Jenna said, grinning from ear to ear.

What on earth would she do with a dog? Except perhaps love it. And since she didn't get the captain's job, maybe she should spend more time at home and less time on her career. Mandy said a quick prayer in her head, wanting guidance.

The puppy licked her chin. A gesture that felt like a divine nudge. "Okay," she said at last, resigned to the fact this didn't go as planned. But then, some of the best things that happened in life were unplanned.

"Really?" Jenna asked, unable to contain her grin.

"Yes," Mandy said, forcing the words out that would change her life. A puppy. A puppy that would grow into a much bigger dog. Not in a million years would she have guessed the outcome from stopping at the park. And the more she thought about it, the more she realized it would be okay.

"Great. Now that we have that settled, how about introducing me to the new captain?"

"Jenna, this is Captain Liam Carter, the newest addition to the department I've been telling you about. Liam, this is my best friend Jenna."

"Nice to meet you. I've heard so much about you," Jenna said.

"Nice to meet you as well. I'm sure what you heard has been nothing good, but in my defense, I didn't know I was taking Mandy's job when I accepted the promotion."

"Oh, how's that?" Jenna asked with interest.

"I mean, I knew someone wasn't getting the job. I just didn't know Mandy. It made it easier being an unknown person without a face."

"*Hmmm.* Never thought of it that way. He's right, Mandy."

She didn't want to discuss any of this, especially not in front of Liam. "Okay, you two. Enough with the mutual fan club. I've got to do something with the puppy."

"I can fix that. Hey, Max. You've got a taker," Jenna hollered.

Max moved to stand by Mandy, a lot of other folks turning to smile and offer their congratulations. "Oh, nice. You picked a friendly one, that's for sure. I named her Frieda, but you can change it to anything you want. The puppies have all had their shots, but you'll need to decide if you're going to breed Frieda or get her fixed in the next few months if you don't want more puppies down the road."

"I like the name Frieda. A lot. It was my great grandmother's name." Talk about another sign.

"Sounds like you too were destined for each other," Liam said.

"I second that," Jenna said, petting the puppy.

Max nodded. "Thank you so much, Sergeant Peters. I know Frieda will have a wonderful home with you."

Mandy was still in shock that she'd said yes, and for what came next. "You're welcome. What am I going to do with Frieda now? I'm still on duty." She clearly hadn't thought this through in the impromptu moment.

"We can take her to your place. But first, we'll stop by the hardware store and get a crate and some other necessary puppy supplies. I think you should take the afternoon off and get acclimated to the newest member of your family," Liam offered.

Mandy grinned. "I'd be worried my boss wouldn't take kindly to me skipping out on work."

"Boss's orders," he teased.

"I like the way your boss thinks," Jenna said, unable to stop grinning.

Who was she to fight city hall when it came in the form of her boss, her best friend, and Frieda? "Well, in that case, I accept. And I expect you to help me out when I need help, since this is all new to me. Both of you," she clarified.

"You know I'll help whenever I can, Miss I Won't Fall In Love." Jenna was pleased with herself knowing she'd been right. Mandy had lost the challenge. Perhaps this little bundle of fur was exactly what Mandy needed. The idea of going home to Frieda every night instead of being alone was hitting her with a clarity she hadn't expected. This was the right thing for her to do. She was sure of it.

"It's been twenty years since I've had a dog, but I'll see what I can do," Liam added.

Mandy was surprised. In all their conversations, this wasn't something that had ever come up. "I didn't know you had a dog before."

"I was just a kid, and then I moved away and couldn't take the dog with me. Poncho died a few years later, I heard, but not a day went by that I didn't miss him."

A kid moving away. Piecing it together, it could only mean after the tragic accident when his parents and sister died. "That's sad. I'm sorry. Truly," she said, placing one hand on his arm, hoping to convey the depth of feeling she had for what he'd been through as a young man.

"Thanks. I've made my peace with the past," he said, but the crisp tones of his voice and their earlier discussion told her otherwise. "We should go. It was nice to meet you, Jenna," Liam said, smiling at her friend.

"Likewise. Call me tonight, Mandy. I want to hear how you and Frieda are doing."

"Sure thing. Wish me luck. I'm going to need it, poor puppy."

"You'll be fine." Jenna laughed.

Mandy and Liam made their way back to the patrol car, a to-go bag of goodies and a new puppy in hand. She settled in the front seat, making sure Frieda was comfortable on her lap.

Liam drove to the hardware store, and they headed inside. A place where pets were permitted, which was great, since she wasn't ready to let her new friend out of sight.

Two hundred and twenty-nine dollars later, they headed for her house. Frieda sat contentedly on her lap, falling asleep soon after, as though the whole shopping expedition had tired her out.

Liam followed Mandy's directions and was soon pulling into her driveway. The small, quaint yellow cottage with white trim and a white picket fence didn't match Mandy's outgoing, take-charge personality. It was almost as though there was another side of her she didn't share with others, and it made him even more curious about his partner.

"Nice house. The puppy will have lots of safe areas to run and play," he said, getting out of the car.

Mandy came around the front, Frieda cradled in her arms like a baby. "I like it. I bought it soon after I moved to town. The neighbors are awesome, and of course, everyone loves having a patrol car parked on their street at night. At least they did when I used to bring the car home. Someone else has that privilege now." Mandy laughed.

"Sorry. I could let you have it in the evenings. Wouldn't want an angry mob of neighbors coming after me," he teased. Liam grabbed the puppy chow out of the back seat in one hand, and the kennel crate in another. He headed up the walkway, close on Mandy's heels, after she held the iron gate open for him.

"That's okay. This is a pretty quiet street. I think the average age is fifty-five plus. And that's with me bringing down the curve." Mandy grinned. She cuddled the puppy as she shifted to the left to block his view while she entered the code in her keypad on the front door. Not that she had to worry about him, but it was good that she was cautious, and common sense was second nature. It was another of her excellent police officer qualities.

"Yes, you are just a youngster. How old are you anyway?" he asked, when she pushed open the front door. Call it curiosity or interest, either term worked.

Mandy smiled. "It's not polite to ask a woman her age."

"Hey, you brought up the age thing, not me."

She tilted her head to one side, as if unsure of him. "Does that mean you haven't read my personnel file yet? Interesting But if that's the case, I'm happy to share that I'm thirty-three.

What about you since we're doing a tell all? How old are you?"

"I'm thirty-eight, and I don't care who knows it." Liam chuckled. "You should probably let Frieda run in the yard a bit. It might help tire her out before introducing her to your place, with the bonus of a potty break."

Mandy nodded. "Good idea." She moved to the middle of the front yard and put the puppy in the grass. "Clearly, I don't know the first thing about training a dog."

"I'll help you. After all, I did sort of push you along back there," Liam offered, watching as Frieda ran around the yard, sniffing and smelling everything in sight.

The puppy ran back to Mandy and barked. "Yes, you and Jenna certainly did that, but I admit, I'm more than a little excited now. It might be nice to come home to a companion at night. Someone to talk to." She reached down to pet Frieda for a few seconds before the puppy took off running again. It was as though

Frieda was checking in. The two would make a good team.

"You know the dog can't really talk back to you, right?"

"She can in doggy talk."

Mandy's comment about having someone to talk to sounded like she led a lonely life. He was guessing it was her choice, because any man worth his salt would stand in line for a chance to date such a beautiful woman. "Don't you date?" he couldn't help but ask.

She frowned. "Hardly." Frieda spotted a butterfly and was off and chasing it around the yard, yapping away.

"What's that supposed to mean? Are you afraid to date or have you sworn off dating men after your ex-husband? That's quite a long time." It didn't seem possible. The men around here had to be blind or they didn't have the tenacity to knock down the walls she had erected around her heart.

"Curiosity killed the cat," Mandy quipped, grinning at him.

"It's just a question. Two friends talking about life. It's not like I'm asking you out," he clarified, not wanting to give her the wrong idea.

"Of course you're not asking me out. That would be silly. To answer your rather personal question, it's a combination of both. My friends think I should start dating again, and I have considered it. But it's complicated."

Relationships were hard work, but it did not mean avoiding them at all costs. "Complicated how?" He realized the irony of his question given his own anti-dating thoughts. Despite that, he wanted to know her answer.

"I'm a female police officer, in case you haven't noticed. A lot of men feel threatened by that, though I don't understand why. I'm still just a woman when I come home at night," she said, scooping up Frieda into her arms to snuggle the puppy. A defense posture that spoke volumes.

"I noticed, trust me. And those men are fools. I'd date you if I wasn't your boss," he teased, shooting her a grin. He loved her shocked expression and enjoyed that he could rattle her usual composure.

"Gee thanks. That makes me feel a whole lot better. Good thing you're my boss then, so I wouldn't have to hurt your feelings and tell you no." Mandy rolled her eyes and set Freida back down in the grass, watching as the puppy raced around the yard.

Liam followed. "What? How could you say no to the likes of me?" he asked, feigning shocked disbelief.

Mandy grinned. "Easy. You're not my type."

"What is your type?"

"I don't know, honestly. That's another reason I'm not dating. I didn't do such a good job the first time around."

"Fair enough." They watched the puppy run and play, standing side by side. A comfortable silence settled between them. It was a good time to push forward his agenda on the investigation.

"Being new around here, I was hoping you could fill me in on a few things."

"Like what?"

This is where it got tricky. Asking her opinion about a fellow officer was likely to stir up questions. "Your impression of the other officers on our team, for starters?"

"There's only seven of us and you seem to be in tight with Chief Jackson. The other five guys are hardworking family men who have been on the force for years with the exception of Ethan who just got engaged. Good men who work hard, show up at school events and go to church. Not much else to tell." She was watching him closely, and it was almost as if he could see her brain racing and trying to figure out why he was questioning her.

"So, no one has ever given you cause for concern in the four years you've been here?" he persisted, hoping to rule out the entire CCPD. Her instincts were good, and he trusted her. It was true. Somewhere along the line, he'd ruled her out as a suspect.

"Why are you asking? This sounds like you're digging for information. Or dirt," she added.

Time to back off the line of questioning and redirect it outside of the CCPD. Police officers liked to protect their own. "Neither. I'm just trying to get to know and understand the people I'm responsible for. It is easier to ask you than read their HR files. Files don't always tell you what you need to know about someone."

Her brow scrunched up, the lines deepening into grooves. "You have a good team, Liam. The only qualms we all have are still trying to figure out who paid who off to get you the captain's job."

"Touche." She was quick witted and sharp as a tack. "Okay, thanks for the information. What about some of the other police departments you've had the occasion to work with? Like the officers in Wylie and Fontana? Is there anybody you don't like or have had trouble with in the past?"

Mandy shook her head. "Now I know you're asking these questions for a reason, and I want to know why?" she demanded.

"Does everything have to have a reason?" It should, but he wasn't about to tell her that. That was just good police business.

"Yes," she said, her voice flat and decisive.

"I'm just asking to know your opinion. It helps me to understand the area. That's all," Liam added, trying to diffuse the tension.

"Fine. Not that I'm buying your lame excuse."

"And..." he prompted, spurring her on to answer when she didn't come right out and start talking.

Mandy folded her arms and watched Frieda run around, not bothering to look at him at all. "It's not that often we cross paths. When we do, the guys seem all right. There's one woman in the Fontana department, and she's married with children. The Wylie PD has been pretty overworked ever since the last big case, especially since one officer just lost his wife to cancer and they are short-handed. We all keep our eyes and ears open in case some tidbit drops in our laps. But they haven't appealed to us to step in any more than we did when the...when the crime was first committed. I figure they simply want to handle their own investigation, though I hear the Texas Department of Public Safety is getting involved."

Liam knew first-hand that the DPS involvement extended to the Texas Rangers, not that he was inclined to share that information. He couldn't help but notice that once again, Mandy avoided the word kidnapping. "I hadn't heard that. Would be good."

"I agree. Anything to stop the criminals from striking again." Mandy shuddered, lost in her own thoughts.

More proof she wasn't involved, but it didn't explain her aversion to discussing the kidnapping case other than what she already explained. Losing her daughter and the never-ending grief was understandable, but not to the extent of associating with the parents of the kidnapped children at the level she was experiencing.

There was more to the story of her reaction and he hoped someday she would trust him enough to explain.

Mandy scooped the puppy up in her arms. "I'm going to take Frieda inside. Any chance you can bring in the rest of the stuff before you head out? I don't want to leave her alone for even a second until I've had a chance to puppy proof the place."

It was the nicest way to tell him to get lost. Liam would take the hint. "Sure enough." He headed back to the car and carried in everything. He handed Mandy a separate bag. "Here, this is for you. It's a new puppy-mommy present."

Mandy looked up at him in surprise. "You got me a gift?"

Liam smiled. "It would seem so. Figure you might need this right about now."

Mandy pulled a book out of the bag. *Dog Training for Dummies.* "This is perfect, though I hope you're not calling me a dummy." Her smile was firmly back in place, and he was more than a little relieved, as Liam didn't like unnecessary tension between them.

It was almost like fighting with your best friend. "Hardly. It's not like I can change the name of the book to *Dog Training for Smart People Who Never Had A Dog*." Liam chuckled.

"True. Thank you. I didn't even think about getting a book. Just everything else from a leash and collar to puppy pads, toys and food." Mandy laughed.

"You're welcome. Call me if you need anything," Liam said, heading for the door.

"Thanks. I will. I appreciate you giving me the afternoon off. Just know that it doesn't change my curiosity about who you are and why you are here."

Liam saluted her. "I wouldn't expect it to, Sergeant Peters. Enjoy the rest of your evening and your new puppy," he said, waving back at her as he headed out the front door.

Chapter Nine

♥

AFTER TAKING A COUPLE of vacation days to bond with Frieda, Mandy felt comfortable returning to work and leaving the puppy alone for short periods. Chief Jackson had been more than accommodating on the impromptu time off since she rarely used any of her days off. And as for Liam, he had no room to say a thing considering he was a part of the reason she had the puppy in the first place.

The plan was to stop at the house a couple of times during the day, and luckily, her job made it possible. Weekends would be easy, given most of the time she was off duty those days based on her seniority. Frieda seemed content in the crate, complete with a blanket, a stuffed animal, and a chew toy. Frieda's soft brown eyes watched her with trust as Mandy closed the crate door. A new, unexpected feeling caught her off guard. Frieda had snuck into her heart in a big way. This was something she should have done sooner...or more likely, this was the way it should be. God's timing, she realized, was perfect—she didn't want any other dog, she wanted Frieda.

The thought of seeing Liam at the office sent butterflies through her stomach. Mandy hadn't been able to forget his comment about dating her. Try as she might to keep her emotional walls up, his genuine kindness made it difficult. The way he helped with Frieda, his friendly banter with folks in town, his thoroughness on the job. He wasn't lax in his duties, which was the opposite of the way he'd come across in the beginning.

Mandy pulled into her usual spot at the department building. Her steps were light, a reflection of her heart. And she had Frieda, Jenna, and Liam to thank for it.

"Good morning, Edith," she said, stopping at the receptionist's desk to talk to her friend.

"Good morning, Mandy!" Edith said, her always cheerful voice filling the lobby. "Good to have you back. Did you enjoy your time off?"

"I did," Mandy said, already reaching for her phone with an eagerness she once reserved for case files. "I'm sure you heard about my new puppy. She's the cutest border collie-golden retriever puppy ever. Look," Mandy said, opening her phone and showing off several photos. More like a dozen. Each photo captured Frieda in various states of adorable mischief—sleeping with her paws in the air, chasing her tail, snuggling with her new toys. It was like a proud parent showing off pictures of their children to anyone who showed interest.

"Oh, she's a doll. And I love her name. I didn't take you for a dog lover," Edith said, scrolling through each photo with oohs and aahs.

"Neither did I." Mandy chuckled. "Apparently, I'm not as much of a stick in the mud as everyone thinks, myself included." Edith handed back her phone and Mandy headed for her desk.

While sorting through her messages, she sensed someone behind her and turned around, fully expecting it to be Liam. Her sense of disappointment at seeing Officer Smith wasn't lost on Mandy. She would need to rein in her emotions if she didn't want the entire office to know she had a crush on her new boss. "What's happening, Greg?"

"Nice to see you back at work." His gentle smile reached his eyes as he leaned against her desk. "You don't normally take time off, so it came as a shock to everyone." Greg was one of the guys who didn't mind a woman on the force. Not everyone had the same opinion.

"Anything exciting going on around here?"

He shrugged. "Not so much as exciting, but definitely of interest," Greg said, lowering his voice.

Mandy leaned in closer, wondering what could have possibly happened in the short time she was gone. "What's up?"

Greg glanced around, his eyes sweeping the nearly empty office. "You know how we all questioned Captain Carter's sudden appearance?"

"Yes, but I figured that was old news now that he's settled in. I'm over it for the time being," she said, absently twirling her pen as she spoke, knowing she had promised Chief Jackson three weeks. Though what would change was beyond her, until then, she would play nice and stick around.

"There's something else you should know about our new captain. While you were out of the office, Captain Carter spent time going to the Wylie and Fontana police departments. A couple of the guys called over here asking questions about him afterwards."

A small knot formed in her stomach. Mandy couldn't believe Liam would do something like that. "Why would he go visit them?"

Greg shrugged. "Claims he wanted to introduce himself. But from what I hear, he's poking around about the kidnapping case and questioning the handling of the paperwork at the Wylie PD. They don't trust him. You're his partner, is there anything suspicious going on with the guy in your opinion? They are wondering if he's showboating his new power position or if he's got political reasons for sticking his nose in where it doesn't belong."

Liam's excuse was plausible, but he had just asked for Mandy's opinion about the other officers in Wylie and Fontana PDs, and that should have been enough. She wrapped her arms around herself, trying to ward off a chill that had nothing to do with the office temperature. There was something going on and she was more determined than ever to figure it out. Not that she'd say anything to anyone else about her suspicions. At least, not yet.

If there was something afoot she would be there right next to him, watching his every move. "No, nothing suspicious. Like I said, I trust him. We're friends, or so I think."

"That's odd, considering he took your job," Greg said, his forehead creasing with concern.

Mandy straightened in her chair, squaring her shoulders. She would need to be careful to cover her feelings about the new captain. Especially since she wasn't sure how she felt. "What else am I supposed to do? Go cry about it? Let's be real. Any guy on the force would deal with the situation the same way I am."

Greg nodded, his shoulders relaxing as the tension left him. "I reckon. Just keep an eye on the captain and let us know if you find anything out. No one else is quite ready to fully trust the rookie officer boss."

"I understand." She fiddled with her necklace, a nervous habit she developed over the years, the cross pendant bringing comfort. She didn't want to trust Liam, but she did. Mostly because she trusted her instincts. It wasn't his fault he took her job. Like he told

Jenna, it wasn't personal because he never knew her.

Greg walked away, obviously unsettled by her responses. It was not like she ever engaged in office gossip, and she wouldn't start now.

Mandy made her way to Chief Jackson's office and closed the door, the familiar scent of his personal coffee pot brewing. "Got a minute?"

The chief sat back in his chair, dropping his pen on the desk. "Sure. What's up?"

"Captain Carter is up to something. He's poking his nose in the recent Wylie case where it doesn't belong. The others are suspicious and looking for answers. As am I." She stayed standing, her fingers drumming against her thigh as she watched his reaction. It was worth a shot to toss out feelers and see if they landed.

The chief shook his head. "Let it go, Sergeant Peters. He's a good man and not up to anything but his job. Quit listening to the whining going on around here. The new captain has been pushing everyone to clean up their files and he's going through some of the older files as a means of reviewing the quality of their paperwork. They aren't too happy with the extra hours or being under scrutiny."

Mandy blinked in surprise. "Oh," she said, her voice softening. "Is that what their sudden interest is about?"

"Yes. So how are things going between the two of you? Are you still mad at me for partnering you together?"

She shifted weight from one foot to the other, choosing her words carefully. Mandy wasn't about to fold under his intense scrutiny, but she would hide her feelings, unwilling to give him reason to question her protocol. "He's alright. I don't want to like him, but I do," she admitted begrudgingly. "You're down to two weeks, though, and we both know there's nothing you can do to fix this. I need to think about my future."

The chief nodded. "Trust me, I'm well aware the clock is ticking. I'm working on it, I promise. And thanks for giving Captain

Carter a chance. The others aren't so fond of the guy."

"He has to earn his place. In time, it will happen." Mandy stood and moved to the door. "Thanks for listening."

Back at her desk, the silence in the room was broken only by the steady ticking of the wall clock and the occasional hum of the air conditioning. It was a rare moment and one she wanted to enjoy. She skimmed through the photos of Frieda and smiled. A shadow fell across her desk and she looked up to find Liam standing there, her heart skipping a beat. She tried not to let her happiness at seeing him show externally.

"Good morning. Glad to have you back, partner," Liam said, leaning against her desk in a casual pose.

"Thanks. It's good to be back. Though I miss Frieda. I'm hoping we can stop by the house a couple of times today."

"Of course. How's she adjusting to her new home? And how are you adjusting to being a dog owner?

Mandy smiled. "Freida's spoiled, but I can't help myself. Soon enough, I'll get down to being a little stricter. Just not yet. She's so stinkin' cute and when she looks at me with those puppy eyes, I melt."

Liam laughed. "It'll be fine. Dogs do best starting the more basic command training around six months old. This is the time to have fun and play. Ready to go?"

"Sure thing. Let me just grab my sweater from the locker room. I'll meet you out front."

The silence in the patrol car felt heavy, as conversation was almost non-existent and it was driving Mandy crazy. She wanted to ask him questions, trying to glean information why he was so interested in the Wylie kidnapping case. "I heard you visited our neighboring police departments," she said, opting to be direct. It was the only way to get answers.

Liam's gaze landed on her and he nodded. "I did. Word travels fast."

"It's Crossroads Creek, not Dallas." Mandy chuckled, watching his profile as he drove. "Learn anything good?" she asked, trying her best to sound nonchalant.

"No. I was just introducing myself," Liam said, unwilling to give her anything more.

"So I heard, but there's talk that some of your direct questions made the Wylie PD uncomfortable. They think you disapprove of the way they are handling the recent case and are here to make trouble for them. Are you trying to make them look bad, and by virtue of that, make yourself look good? Or perhaps you're here for political reasons which would explain you getting the promotion out of nowhere."

"They're wrong," Liam said, his deadpan tone resolute.

It was an uphill battle trying to get him to tell her anything. "Could you be more forthcoming?"

"No." His jaw tightened, the muscle twitching slightly. End of that discussion. *Clearly*.

"Well, okay then. Will you answer me another question?" Mandy asked, trying to figure out something about Liam she didn't already know.

"Depends on what it is."

"The other day, you were full of many questions about my dating habits or the lack thereof. What about you? Why aren't you dating again? Or are you? And why did you want to move here...in the middle of nowhere?" She held her breath, waiting for his response. It was her roundabout way to find out what she needed to know about this man. It wouldn't do her any good to keep thinking about him and his dating comment if he was already attached to someone.

"I don't date. In my line of work, every day can present dangers. I don't want that to extend to a family."

"Our line of work, you mean?" She turned slightly in her seat to face him. Or was it only because she was a woman that it was supposed to be a different set of dating rules for her?

"*Ummm*, yes. That's what I meant," Liam corrected, running a hand through his sandy-blond hair as though unnerved by her line of questioning.

Mandy nodded. "I get it, but then why did you tell me that I should date again?"

"I don't have an appropriate answer for that."

"Because I'm a woman?" she pressed, addressing the obvious issue at hand.

His fingers tightened on the steering wheel. Liam shook his head. "No. Because you deserve to be loved." He kept his eyes on the road as he delivered the bomb.

"And you don't?" she asked, her voice softening with concern.

Liam sucked in a deep breath. "No."

The pain in that single word made her heart ache. "Explain it to me, please. I'm trying to understand, and it's like getting water out of a dry well with you." Mandy didn't know what else to do to get him to trust her. To open up. She knew this was about his past, but unless he shared, she couldn't help him. And she wanted to. The same way he wanted to help her.

"I don't talk about the past with anyone," Liam said, still shutting her out.

"I'm not anyone. I'm your partner."

"True." His fingers tapped rapidly against the steering wheel. "Do you remember when I told you about my family dying in a car accident?" Liam pulled to the side of the road and parked.

"Yes."

He turned, watching her closely. "I also told you folks blamed me. What I didn't tell you was the reason they felt that way. I was supposed to watch my sister, but I had some trouble at school and headed to a special place I liked to go when I needed to be alone and sort things out. I fell asleep, and I was an hour late getting home. My parents had an appointment in Dallas and were late leaving and had to take my sister with them. If I hadn't been late, they wouldn't have been where they were when the drunk driver hit them and none of them would have died."

Mandy froze, her brain going in a million directions, her throat tight. Talk about a heavy load of guilt for something out of his control. She reached for his arm, the need to comfort him overwhelming her professional boundaries. "You're wrong to feel guilty. You were a kid trying to deal with your own issues, which let's face it...being a kid isn't easy. The guilt lies with the drunk driver. That's who is responsible for the accident and the heartbreaking tragic deaths of your family. What if you were sick in the nurse's office and were late? Would you still be guilty? What if you were driving home and your car broke down? Does that make you guilty? I can name you so many things, but the answer is always no in case you can't figure that out. You aren't responsible. A kid being late for something, that might be cause for a grounding or taking away their phone or xbox. Not condemned as guilty for the rest of their lives for something they didn't do.

And did you ever consider that maybe your parents were late leaving for other reasons, like the car wouldn't start. They could have left ten minutes after you were late. Or twelve minutes. Or twenty. Every minute difference changes the outcome. You didn't dictate when they left the house. You can't play the what-if game and spend the rest of your life feeling guilty for something that is not your fault."

Liam let out a huge sigh. "I don't know any other way."

She was trying to reach but failing miserably. "We should pray about this. Together."

"I stopped praying a long time ago," Liam said, rubbing the back of his neck.

Mandy leaned in closer. "Then it's time you started again. It's the only thing that has seen me through my darkest days."

Liam reached for her hand, his warm fingers wrapping around hers. It was almost as if he wanted her to pray and he was hoping for a shred of light, a moment of relief from his pain. *Lord, let the words of healing come naturally.*

She bowed her head and prayed, the connection a strong bond between them. Two people in prayer fighting back against years of guilt. Something she was all too familiar with. Afterward, they sat in silence. She searched for the right words to comfort him, and she knew it was time she shared her story. Liam trusted her with his deepest secret, and it was time she did the same with him. Her heart pounded against her ribs as she gathered courage. "I understand guilt. I'd like to share something with you about me that no one else knows. I'm trusting you with the truth about something I did, or didn't do, but I prefer this to remain a secret."

"I'm listening. You have my word what you tell me shall remain between us," Liam said, his voice solemn.

Her hands trembled in his grip. Mandy swallowed hard, searching for the right words. What if he lost respect or hated her knowing the truth? Perhaps this, too, was part of her healing process. To trust someone with the truth. "You know when I told you about my daughter and how I lost her eight years ago?"

"Yes."

"You assumed my daughter died, and I let you believe that. Olivia didn't die. She was kidnapped." The words hung heavily in the air between them. That part of her story was common knowledge if he had read her files. It was the rest of the story that never let her forget her part in what happened the night she was kidnapped.

"Oh, Mandy..." he said, his voice gentle and filled with sympathy. "You should have told me before. I would never have pushed you about the Wylie case. I'm so sorry. Can you tell me what happened? You're trying to help me, so perhaps it's time we helped each other."

She stared out the windshield, focusing on a distant tree as the memories washed over her. Mandy knew it was time to catch Liam up on the whole story. "I was living in Austin and going to law school. My daughter was one week old. One night, I was so tired and went to bed early. I thought I heard something, but I couldn't move. I was so exhausted. She wasn't crying, so I thought she had to be okay, and that I was paranoid. I knew John would be home late, but that he would check on Olivia. I fell back asleep and didn't wake until John started yelling at me. Earlier that day when we talked, he kept telling me I needed to get more sleep and that when he got home, he'd make sure I finally got a good night's rest and got caught up."

Liam nodded in understanding. "That's normal after delivering a baby. It's a big adjustment. But go on."

"That's it. I heard a noise and didn't respond to my baby." Her voice cracked on the last word, years of pain bleeding through. She couldn't bring herself to tell him the last detail. It was just too much, and she couldn't bear to see the questioning look in his eyes, the way the other police officers had made her feel. *Guilty.*

The patrol car felt too small, and too intimate, as Liam reached out to touch her face. "I'm sorry. That's a load of guilt no one should have to bear. I'll throw your words back at you. It's not your fault. Even if you had gotten up, the kidnappers would have waited until the coast was clear. There was nothing you could do to stop the evil unleashed in your home. It's not your fault, it's the kidnappers."

He was right. Except she hadn't told him the one piece that might change his mind about her forever. Lost in her misery, she didn't realize Liam had closed the distance between them until it was too late. His lips softly touched hers.

The gentle press of his lips sent warmth spreading through her chest, a stark contrast to the cold guilt she'd been carrying. She savored the moment for a few seconds, before pulling back, her fingertips going to her lips. From despair to a feeling of what? Happiness? It wasn't possible, and yet there was no other way to explain the sudden warmth in her heart. "That shouldn't have happened. You're my boss." Not that Mardy would have changed any part of the moment.

Liam touched her chin and forced her to look at him. "Perhaps. But you're also a woman with a lot of emotional pain and I wanted to give you a moment of comfort."

"That's sweet of you." She blinked back unexpected tears. The problem was the connection and comfort she felt was something she hadn't felt in years...if ever. She wanted desperately to tell Liam the rest of her story, but she couldn't bring herself to trust him with the final piece of information yet.

The rest of their shift went routinely with conversation focused on police matters. Meal breaks were much quieter, the silence between them charged with unspoken words from their earlier discussion. Liam was grateful for the respite, wanting time to process the exchange when he was alone this evening. Mandy's comforting words made sense, but letting go of the guilt wasn't that simple. Though he had to admit, her prayer had brought him a moment of comfort.

There was also the information she dropped like a bomb in his lap, information that could be vital to his investigation. His heart ached for her pain, and the kiss had been an instinctive response to comfort her. It was only after the kiss he realized the significance of what she told him.

Liam had reviewed her Austin PD and Crossroads Creek PD personnel files and her service was exemplary. By not going back to a time before she became a police officer, he'd missed the fact her daughter had been kidnapped. It explained so many of her reactions to his comments.

The weight of her revelation was heavy on Liam, making him eager to get back to the office and follow up on this lead. Was her daughter's kidnapping related to the kidnapping ring? The timing was off, but close enough to consider. Luckily, he had the Texas Rangers' authority and could get any information he wanted with the proper documentation and sound reasoning.

Suddenly Mandy was tied to his case in more ways than he cared to admit, yet he couldn't say anything to her about it. Especially since it was also clear to him he cared about her more than he should.

Chapter Ten

♥

AFTER A DAY OF driving around town and nothing but routine calls, Liam and Mandy returned to the office to work on an endless stack of tasks, including her share of the planning for the annual bachelor auction scheduled in two months' time. When she had first mentioned it to Liam, his expression had darkened, and he hadn't been overly excited at the details. Once she explained that the folks in town wouldn't take too kindly to their new captain, who was a bachelor, brushing off such an important event, he resigned himself to the inevitable. A minimum bid of two hundred dollars would get an eight-hour day of labor, or whatever else the winning bidder wanted, within legal reason, of course.

It was all for a good cause...funding for the community center's free food night on Wednesdays. Something Liam had yet to attend, as she pointedly mentioned during the morning briefing, earning her an eye roll from her new boss.

"Want to get a pizza after work?" Liam asked, leaning against her desk with a calm confidence.

Mandy nodded, trying not to read more into it than a chance for two people who worked together to grab some food. "Sure thing. Remember, I skipped lunch to run errands and take care of Frieda. Not enough time in a lunch hour to get it all done. Unless the boss would care to give me extra time," she added, grinning up at Liam, trying to ignore his cologne, a subtle mix of cedar and spice she wholeheartedly enjoyed.

"Nice try. And here I thought you were eating at home to save money," he teased, his dark-chocolate eyes sparkling with merriment.

"Well, if you want to increase my salary...feel free." Mandy grinned, grabbing a file on her desk as she stood, the top of her head barely reaching his chin. Liam was tall, with broad shoulders and an athletic build, which made him an imposing figure. *Exactly what one would want in a captain.*

"I'll see what I can do. No promises."

She hadn't actually been serious, but she wouldn't say no. It would help make up for some of what she lost when he stole her job. "Well, then. I've got to copy this file and drop off a report to the Chief. Give me about twenty minutes."

"Sounds good." Liam strode away, his confident stride and well-fitting uniform pants hard not to notice.

"What are you staring at Mandy?" Edith asked, her eyes dancing with mischief.

Mandy's chin rose a notch in defense, the heat of a flush spreading across her cheeks and down her throat. "I'm not staring at anything."

"Horse feathers." Edith's laughter rang out in the office. "But he's a good-looking guy and there is no harm in looking. You two sure are getting along better than anyone expected. Is there romance in the air?" she asked without hesitation.

Mandy shook her head and frowned, while her heart skipped an unwanted beat. It wouldn't do for anyone to suspect her developing feelings went beyond working partners. Least of all Edith. She was a friend, but she loved to talk and share juicy gossip if she thought something was important. "Hardly. He's my boss, and that would be against company policy."

Edith shrugged and leaned forward. "I suppose, but it sure doesn't hurt to look...or dream," she said, her voice low enough to keep it a private comment.

"If you say so," Mandy said, forcing a casualness into her voice she didn't feel. The last thing she needed was the office rumor mill linking her and Liam romantically.

"Anyway, do you want to get a bite to eat after work? Tom and the kids are going to his mother's place, and he wanted me to have a night off. A rare treat," Edith added.

It would have been nice to have a girl's night out. It wasn't often she had the time, and when she did, it was rarely used for socializing. At least not until Liam showed up in town. "Sorry, I've already got plans." Except her plans weren't a date and three wouldn't be a crowd. In fact, three would keep folks in town from speculating. "I have a better idea. Why don't you join us for pizza at Mario's?"

"Us?"

"Liam and me. We're headed over to the pub after our shift."

Edith grinned, one eyebrow raised in doubt. "Is that a fact? Like I said, you two are awfully chummy."

"Not at all, which is why I'm insisting you come. Then you can see for yourself and help

squash any ridiculous rumors to the contrary."
Mandy should have thought through either
decision better. Dinner alone with Liam was a
sure-fire way to garner hot-off-the-press gossip attention, and asking the town gossip to
join them was playing with fire.

Edith nodded. "Well, okay then. If you're
sure I won't be a third wheel. Beats sitting
home alone tonight."

"Great, we're leaving in about fifteen minutes," Mandy said, knowing the time was ticking, and she needed to hurry to finish what she
had to do. It wouldn't do to leave Liam hanging
out by the front door, telling everyone who he
was waiting on.

"I'll be ready," Edith confirmed.

Mandy made her way to the archaic copy
machine and prayed it wouldn't give her any
trouble. The chief wanted this on his desk
before she left, and he always got what he
wanted. She learned that early on when she'd
forgotten something and her head was on the
chopping block for five minutes at the next

morning briefing. She vowed to never make that mistake again.

Right on schedule, they all left for the pizza parlor. Liam didn't seem to care one bit that Edith was going to tag along. Unfortunately, Mandy couldn't decide if that was a bad or a good thing. Her fingers drifted to her lips as she remembered the kiss. It changed everything between them, and she hadn't been able to get it out of her mind.

The bells jingled overhead as they walked into Mario's, the aroma of fresh-baked dough and pizza cooking in the brick oven, making her hungry. "Grab a seat and I'll be right with you," Tina called out from behind the counter where she was tossing pizza dough into the air with an artistic flair that spoke of years of practice.

"Thanks." Mandy led them to one of the corner tables and pulled out a wooden chair, leaving the booth bench for the others if they wanted it. Sitting that close to Liam would be difficult at best. Liam and Edith settled in across from her and then picked up menus.

"What's good here?" Liam asked.

"Pizza," Mandy quipped, shooting him a grin.

"Haha. I'm serious. What do you ladies like best?" Liam asked, rephrasing the question as he studied the laminated menu.

"Hawaiian is my favorite. Any takers?" Edith said, looking at them to see if anyone would agree.

"Yuk. Pineapple on a pizza is like unconstitutional or something," Liam teased, his nose wrinkling in mock disgust.

Edith rolled her eyes. "Let me guess, you're a meat lover supreme all the way?"

Liam shook his head to the contrary. "No. Just not a fruit lover on pizza Or anchovies, for that matter," he added.

"Okay, so no fruit or anchovies. We can do this. I'm good with pepperoni, olives, and onion. Does that work for everyone?" Mandy asked, trying to find something that balanced a protein and veggies.

"Absolutely," Liam said, happy to agree.

Edith shrugged. "I suppose. Unless you can get them to slide a couple of pineapple chunks on two of the slices."

Mandy bit back a smile. She was clearly trying to be difficult on purpose, testing the waters with the new guy in town. It was most comical, but it wouldn't get dinner ordered and her rumbling stomach was getting louder. "I'll see what Tina can do," Mandy said, searching the room for their server.

Country music drifted from the jukebox in the corner, mixing with the cheerful buzz of conversation—typical of small-town Friday night fun. A time when everyone liked to relax and cut loose.

"What can I get you all?" Tina asked, pulling a pen from her curly hair and retrieving a pad from her apron.

"A large pepperoni, olives, and onions, please. Oh, and pineapple chunks on two slices if you can, please."

"Pineapple's fine for an extra dollar," Tina said, as she pulled the pen tucked behind her ear and flipped open her order pad and began jotting down the order.

"That's fine, and thank you," Edith said, happier now that she got her way to some extent.

"And for drinks?" Tina asked, pen poised over the pad.

"I'll have an iced tea please," Mandy said.

"Same for me, but unsweetened," Liam added, surprising Mandy with the sugar-free choice, making her wonder what other surprises he held.

"I'll have a Pepsi," Edith chimed in.

"Got it. It'll be about twenty minutes on the pizza, and I'll bring some garlic bread sticks out in a second. Anything else?" Tina asked, already stepping back as another table waved for her attention.

"No, that's it. Thanks," Mandy said, smiling at the server who was hustling tonight with a full crowd.

"That worked out well. Glad you could be accommodated, Edith." Liam grinned and bumped her shoulder with her in a friendly gesture. "So, tell me ladies, what else is there to do in town besides eat and work?"

"There's always something going on. We have a bachelor auction for charity that's coming up soon. Something you could sign up for, just saying," Edith said, her eyes sparkling with mischief as she tried to pin Liam down to volunteer.

"Yes, I've heard all about the auction. It's not my thing, but Mandy tells me it would look bad if I don't go as the new guy in town." Liam shifted uncomfortably and looked at Edith like a man searching for an escape route. Most likely hoping she'd tell him it was no big deal.

"She's not wrong," Edith confirmed.

Liam shook his head, resignation written on his face. "Then I guess I'm in, unless anything changes between now and then."

"Like what?" Mandy challenged.

"I could get hurt in the line of duty. You know, like a broken arm. Or shot." His lips twitched as he fought a smile.

"I didn't take you for a drama king," she teased. "It's not that bad, I promise. You might mow a lawn or paint a fence. It builds character," Mandy said, enjoying his discomfort a bit too much.

"If you say so." Liam didn't look convinced.

The Friday night crowd filled every table and booth, with the overflow gathering round the bar. The noise made it hard to have a conversation without raising one's voice and leaning in closer. "There's also an occasional dance. And don't forget the Wednesday night thing where everyone eats free at the community center. The whole town turns out so it would be a great place to meet people," Mandy offered.

"And we have a few festivals during some holidays," Edith added, warming to the topic.

"Regular busy town." Liam chuckled.

"Don't laugh. It can be fun if you're a joiner. Don't knock it until you've been to a few events," Mandy added.

"It's not like you go either," Edith said, calling her out.

"That's because I was working and you know it," she said, defending her choice.

"So, what's next?" Liam asked.

"There's an annual line-dancing event in three weeks at the community center. Everyone brings their favorite food dish and learns new country line dances," Mandy said.

"Are you asking me?" Liam's expression shifted from teasing to serious as his eyes locked with hers.

Her heart skipped a beat. He was serious...but she wasn't. Or couldn't be. "Hardly."

"Well, that's not very sociable," he quipped.

"I'm having dinner at my mother's that night, so I'm out. But it is so much fun. You really should try it, Captain Carter," Edith said, leaning in even closer to him.

"Call me Liam when we're off duty. And seeing as I don't know any line dances, it's a hard pass for me as well."

"People go to learn. You know how to learn, right?" Edith chuckled.

"If he's as good on two feet as he is at the office, we are all in trouble. Talk about stomping on toes," Mandy chimed, unable to resist teasing him.

Liam threw his head back and laughed, the rich sound drawing looks from nearby guests. "Hey, I resemble that remark. If I go, are you coming with me?" he asked, throwing out the challenge and catching Mandy off guard. He had stomped on a few toes but it was all for good cause.

"You're my boss," she said, reminding him of the cold hard facts, even though her heart had a mind of its own.

"Great. Then I'm ordering you to go with me, so that I don't make a fool of myself in front of everyone looking like a lonesome loser. All eyes will be on you."

Mandy's heart raced at the thought of dancing with Liam. Line dances would be fun, but what if they played a slow song? She'd be in his arms for all of three minutes, but the very idea made her feel giddy like a schoolchild. "Then I guess I don't have a choice, since it's an order."

Liam nodded. "Then I guess I'm in, seeing as you're being so accommodating." His phone rang. He glanced at the screen, his entire expression transformed, softening into a smile she'd never seen before—one that revealed a glimpse of his carefully guarded heart.

"Hey there, what's up?" Liam said, turning slightly away to hear better. "I see. That's not good. I wish I had known sooner, but no worries. I'll meet you at the park in about five minutes." He hung up and pocketed the phone. "Sorry ladies, I've got to take a rain check on the pizza. A friend just stopped in town, and I've got to run. Here's a twenty to cover my share of the tab and then some," he said, dropping the money on the red and white checkered tablecloth.

"Hope everything is okay?" Mandy asked, trying to mask her worry and disappointment as curiosity kicked into overdrive.

"Me too." And without another word, Liam left the restaurant in a hurry.

"Interesting," Edith said, frowning as she watched his retreating figure.

"Not really." Actually, it was more than interesting considering she didn't realize he knew anyone in town, and that no one had visited him from Dallas since he landed in Crossroads Creek. Who was this mystery friend that could pull him away with just a phone call?

"Oh well, that's more pizza for us. His loss. But Mandy, you aren't fooling anyone, least of all me." Edith grinned.

"I don't know what you mean," Mandy said, fidgeting with her napkin to avoid her friend's perceptive gaze.

"You like Liam. And the fact he asked you to dinner tonight means he likes you too. It's not like people who work together don't date. The department frowns on it, but it happens anyway. I should know." Edith patted her hand in a show of support, her wedding ring catching the overhead light.

"Do tell," Mandy said, leaning forward to listen as she hadn't heard this story before.

Edith sat back in the booth, her eyes taking on a dreamy quality as she recalled what happened. "A little over nine years ago, I dated one of the officers who worked here. The chief didn't like it, but he didn't put an end to it."

"What happened?" Mandy asked, her friend full of surprises.

"I married him," Edith chuckled, her face radiating joy. "He quit and started working from home doing a landscaping design business. We wanted one of us home with the kids when they came along, and it's worked out great ever since."

Mandy's mouth dropped open, unable to hold her surprise. "You never told me this. Why?"

Edith shrugged, taking a sip of her Pepsi. "We don't talk about the good-ole days much. There's simply too much happening now that's far more important. Like the fact that I'm pregnant again," Edith said, her voice an excited whisper.

"No way. Really? Like seriously?" Mandy couldn't believe it. An all-too-familiar ache bloomed in her chest, followed immediately by a hint of guilt. Edith had it all. A loving husband. Two children. And one on the way. Most of all, she was happy.

"Yes. We weren't planning to have more children. The thing is, I just found out and I haven't told Tom yet." Her hand drifted to her still-flat stomach. "It's a blessing from God and I hope he feels the same way as I do."

"He loves you and he loves God. So, I'm pretty positive he's going to love the baby. Congratulations." Mandy was truly happy for her co-worker, who had also been a good friend for the past few years.

Edith smiled, her eyes glazing over with tears of joy. "Thanks. Now we need to find you someone to start your happily ever after."

Mandy laughed, the sound hollow to her own ears. "My happily ever after ended when Liam swooped in and stole my job. That's what I wanted, and now it's not even remotely possible." No matter what strings Chief Jackson tried to pull. Inevitably, when her three weeks were up, she would leave the CCPD.

"Or maybe your happily ever after is just starting," Edith said.

Mandy knew what she was hinting at but would never agree, or else Edith would forever be after her to move things along. As Tina approached with their pizza, the aroma of melted cheese and warm pizza filled the air.

What if Edith was right? Maybe God had a different plan for her happiness—one she hadn't even considered.

Chapter Eleven

♥

L IAM HURRIED TOWARDS THE park, unable to squash the disappointment of not getting to spend time with Mandy outside of work but knowing his responsibility towards his late partner's wife and children had to take precedent.

The desire to spend more time with Mandy had come as a surprise. *Ever since the kiss.* A kiss that probably shouldn't have happened, but it did. Was it truly out of sympathy? Or was there a deeper reason...one he never expected? He hadn't cared about a woman this way since he was seventeen, young and dumb, and that had proven disastrous. But he was older now, and Mandy was nothing like Mary.

Mandy carried herself with a quiet strength, her faith and determination clear in all she did. She used those qualities to come to grips with the heartache and grief life had dealt her.

He wanted to ignore the faith factor, but more often than not, he couldn't. Like when she was nervous or worried, her hand would go to the cross pendant she had tucked beneath the collar of her uniform shirt.

Once upon a time, he believed. But look where it got him—alone in life. Mandy was also alone, but her solitude was tinged with hope, while his was like a punishment. It was something to consider. When she'd prayed for him in the car, there was no denying the power of calm that settled between the m. Liam clung to that moment of peace for as long as he could, before it finally departed, leaving him alone again with his guilt.

With Mandy, he wanted more from life. For the moment, it didn't matter as he was her boss. But in a week and a half all that would all change, though what that might mean was beyond him. He was returning to Dallas, and Mandy would still be here in Crossroads Creek. Having never considered a relationship because of the dangers, especially as a Texas Ranger. Mandy was an exception to the rule, because she understood the dangers of the job. But a long-distance relationship would have its own set of problems. And that was only if Mandy was interested, and he had no idea where that stood, though he knew she cared. But caring wasn't enough for a person to seek a committed relationship when they came with unresolved issues, some they both had in spades.

It was a good thing Edith had joined them, making it easier for Liam to leave when Veronica called. That his previous patrol partner's wife, had come to Crossroads Creek, could only mean one thing. *Trouble.* In the three years since Brock died, Veronica hadn't recovered from his death and leaned on Liam heavily as her lifeline. Raising three kids on her own wasn't easy, but there was also an occasional premonition that would hit her that something or someone was watching her and the kids. And Liam took watching over them as a serious responsibility, doing what he could after Brock died and wanting to protect his best friend's family.

The memory of that day still made his stomach clench and his heart ache—his partner killed while off-duty, and it appeared to have been a contract hit, if the word on the street was to be believed. Which is exactly why he was paying attention to Veronica and her premonitions. No one knew why and there was always a chance someone would circle back to the family to get what they wanted unless it began and ended with Brock.

Liam walked at a brisk pace, relieved when he spotted them in the distance by the swing set. The twins were six, and Ethan was eight, and all busy having fun swinging. He scanned the area, looking for anything or anyone that jumped out as unusual or out of place.

"Hey there." Veronica said, as he neared. "Thanks for coming, *Liam.*"

"Not a problem and you know it. It is quite a surprise though," he said, hugging her and waving at the laughing children as they swung higher and higher, their delighted squeals carrying on the wind to reach his ears.

"I'm sorry. I know you're undercover and I swear I wouldn't have come unless I was really worried," Veronica said, her words tumbling out in a rush of anxiety.

Liam put an arm around her shoulder. "It's okay. I know the score and it's why I told you how to find me before I left Dallas. Folks around here know me as Captain Liam Carter, and I need to keep it that way." He trusted Veronica with his career...and his life.

"Captain? Nice." Veronica said, her eyes darting between the children and the surrounding area, much the same way he had done.

"What's going on?" he asked, keeping his voice low and steady despite the tension building in his chest.

Veronica bit her lower lip and let out a heavy sigh. "Maybe I'm just being foolish, because when I'm here with you, I don't have the same overwhelming sense of panic I was feeling back home."

He recognized the spiral of fear that still reared its ugly head occasionally after her husband's death. "Brock and I were partners for over ten years. We are close, like family, so it's understandable. Tell me what's bothering you enough to drive here without so much as a heads up." Liam had to keep her focused.

Veronica nodded, wrapping her arms around herself to keep warm against the evening chill settling in. "You know I've moved three times since Brock died. Each time, it's because I get a strange letter that gives me the creeps, like I'm being watched. It's been a year since they found me, but I got another one in the mail. Liam, I'm tired of running, but I don't know what else to do. At some point, the kids are going to be affected and start asking questions. Questions I can't answer."

Liam's stomach knotted with dread. Whoever was stalking her had found her again. It was his greatest fear that the sender was tied to Brock's death. "Let me see the letter."

Veronica reached into her pocket and pulled out a heavily wrinkled envelope and handed it to him.

Sliding out the letter, Liam was careful to only touch the corners. He was surprised it was handwritten, unlike the others which had been typed.

We have something in common. Our spouses are both dead. Two souls, lost in the world, needing each other. Perhaps it's time we finally met.

"Sounds like a creepy, ardent admirer. I hate your fingerprints are on this, but if it's just yours and mine and the author, my team might figure out the writer's identity if he has a criminal record."

"Do you think this is tied to Brock's death?" she asked, her voice barely above a whisper.

Yes. But there was only one answer he could give. Veronica had been through enough already, and he refused to make matters worse. "No. Perhaps it's best if you stop moving. Maybe it's time to confront this stalker head on, with our full protection, of course. The Texas Rangers always take care of their own. You just need to say the word. That's just my opinion and I'll support any decision you make, but I agree, you can't keep running." What he wanted was to find the person responsible and land them in the slammer for threatening a law enforcement officer's wife and family.

"I know, and you can't imagine how much I appreciate it knowing I've got you to turn too." Veronica sniffed, wiping away the tears that slid down her cheeks.

"I'm not saying turn a blind eye to what's around you. Maybe take the kids on a much-needed vacation. Give me time to look into this letter," Liam said, pulling his handkerchief from his pocket—the habit of carrying one, something he learned from his father. One he never let go, as if it kept him tied to his father emotionally. Something he hadn't realized until now. Mandy was having more impact on him than he realized with her sound reasoning. "What do you think?" he asked when she didn't answer.

"I don't know. I haven't been on a vacation in years. Not since Brock..." Veronica couldn't finish the sentence but he knew what she meant.

"All the more reason to go now," he said, encouraging her, knowing it would be a good thing for her to relax and unwind—somewhere safe. For her to have fun with the kids in an exciting way that brought life into the daily drudgery Veronica had fallen into.

"Hawaii. That's where I want to go," she said, suddenly smiling. "Thanks, Liam. I'm so sorry to bother you when I get all freaked out about things."

"You're human. Give yourself the much-needed change of scenery from Texas. I can get it arranged for you tonight and you can be on a plane by tomorrow."

"I'll do it." Veronica visibly relaxed, having decided.

They stayed at the park, watching the kids play and talking about where she would go and what she would do. Liam would help put her plan into action and felt better knowing she was leaving Dallas, since he wouldn't be back there for a couple more weeks. It was safer this way.

Mandy tucked her credit card back in her wallet and stood. "See you later, Edith. I think I'm going to walk off some of the pizza and then head back to the house to let Frieda out for a run." She patted her full stomach, regretting the third slice but not the laughter that had gone with it. Missing lunch didn't give her stomach more room for extra food, or so it would seem.

Edith nodded. "I've got to get home to the hubby and kids. This was fun. We should do it more often. Maybe I can talk Tom into making this a more regular outing for me, you know, mom's night out." She flung her purse over her shoulder, and they headed for the door. The bell overhead jingled as they stepped out into the cool evening.

"Seems I've got more time on my hands now, so sure." It was fun hanging out with a friend, and something that wasn't work related. Jenna would have enjoyed this as well, so maybe the three of them could start a ladies' night out. It would be a first for Mandy.

Edith headed for her car, and Mandy continued down the street with no destination in mind. The street lights flickered as they turned on, and she was intent on enjoying the beautiful evening. And of course, thinking about Liam.

As if thinking of him, her inner beacon led Mandy to the park. Deep-rooted curiosity, for sure. At first, she didn't see him. Just a couple with their kids embracing. The man tenderly lifted her chin and leaned closer. To kiss her? Mandy was too far away to tell, but a romantic side she didn't know existed seemed to bubble up out of nowhere.

When the two drew apart, that's when she realized the man was Liam. The realization was like a physical blow. A girlfriend? The loving embrace she'd witnessed wasn't two friends hugging, that much she knew. Mandy turned away, having seen enough. She headed back to her car and the solace of her own thoughts.

Liam said he didn't date, and yet, here was proof of his lie. And why keep the woman a se-cret? Now, more than ever, Mandy had to won-der about Liam and his sudden appearance in

Crossroads Creek. She wanted to know what strings were pulled to get him her job...and why. It was time for another chat with Chief Jackson. This time, she wouldn't leave until she had answers.

Or she was leaving CCPD. It was up to Chief Jackson, because one thing she knew for certain, there was no way she would work with a liar as a partner. Especially given the ache in her heart at being played the fool and thinking he cared.

Chapter Twelve

❤

THE HOUSE STILL ECHOED with the warmth of last night's fun and activities.

Liam had gone to the attic and dug out family games long since tucked away in a box. Terrance told him once that he had stored everything in the attic, though Liam never figured to see any of it again as painful reminders of his past. Unable to resist, he also opened the box with his name on it, surprised to find his cowboy hat. With a few stretches to the brim, he made it fit. It felt right, like an old friend coming home when he placed it on his head.

He scanned through the rest of the box, each item bringing back memories. It was then he had spotted the black box. The ring he never gave Mary. He opened the box, the diamond chip all he could afford at the time, stared back at him. He felt nothing. It truly was a blessing they weren't together, as it clearly wasn't meant to be. He snapped the box shut and pocketed the ring, knowing he wanted it gone, and no reminders of the terrible decisions he made as a kid. Falling in love with Mary, being one of them.

With memory lane closed, he called Veronica to help him drag down the box of games. Of course, she teased him about his hat—not that he took it off.

It was on his dresser this morning and the first thing he noticed when he woke up. At least it didn't evoke painful memories, all the more reason to hang on to it. Once a cowboy, always a cowboy.

Veronica and the kids were sleeping in this morning, and he was inclined to let them as they had a big day ahead.

All the reservations were made for their two-week vacation to Hawaii. Luckily, Veronica had brought all of her travel documents with her, not knowing when she would return. There were also several changes of clothes for everyone, though once at her destination, she would need to buy more. He could already picture the kids in bright Hawaiian prints, running along the beach. The thought made him smile.

Movement by the kitchen door drew his attention as Veronica appeared, still rubbing the sleep from her eyes. "Good morning, Veronica. Did you sleep well?" he asked as she headed for the coffee pot.

"Absolutely. I can't believe it's after eight. Aren't you supposed to be at the office already?"

Liam got up to get her a cup and handed it to her. "I am, but I let them know I was running behind. The chief put up a stink, but then what can he do?" He chuckled. It was rare for him not to put the job first. "Loads of fun last night, but I'm dragging a bit," he admitted.

Veronica poured a cup of coffee, the rich aroma drifting his way. She joined Liam at the table, sitting across from him. "Kids will do that to you. Wear you out, that is. So, do you like it here?"

"It suits me just fine for what I'm doing," Liam said.

Veronica's gaze swept the room, and Liam did the same. The morning light revealed the obvious details that needed attending.

"I mean, this place you're renting doesn't quite seem on par with the Liam I know. Bit rustic, not to mention in need of a lot of renovations," she said, watching him closely. "And you must be bored out of your mind in the middle of nowhere."

"It needs work, but it's nothing I can't work on while I'm here. And no, I'm not bored. Seems there's always a lot going on." A smile tugged at his lips. Liam didn't intend to share the pig search, the cat up the tree rescue, or even the fight between neighbors about who got what fruit from the apple tree. It was an annual fight, all based on where the apples fell. Though Mr. Pinkerton felt they were all his since the tree was in his yard. Ornery old coots, but they sure made life interesting. She also didn't know he owned the place or the reason he left and never came back.

"So, when do you go back to Dallas?" Veronica asked, blowing on her coffee to cool it down.

"In a week and a half, give or take a day or so. It just depends on how things are going. So far, I'm not making any progress, but it only takes one lead or break through." Though the thought had crossed his mind that if it took longer, he would talk to his boss and see about sticking around. If he could blame it on Mandy, he would, but it was more than her sweet face. As he went from day to day, and came home at night, he felt a level of settled comfort he hadn't experienced in a long time. *Twenty years, to be exact.*

"You really need to do more than just work. Have you met anyone here, or are you still doing the *all work and no play* lifestyle?"

"I've met a lot of people." Liam chuckled.

"And? Anyone special?" she pressed, studying him over the rim of her cup as she took a sip. Veronica knew him all too well, and that avoidance was the name of the game if she let him.

"Yes. Does that make you happy? She's a police sergeant where I work. The problem is that I'm her boss. And by the time I'm not, I'll be packing to head back to Dallas. No point in starting something I can't finish." On the surface, it all made perfect sense why not to pursue a relationship. It didn't change the stirrings in his heart when he was around her. Especially when he kissed her.

Veronica set her cup down sharply. "Wow. She must be special, as this is a first for you. What's her name?"

"Mandy. But I've already explained to you why it doesn't matter." The words came out sharper than he intended, his defenses on the rise. "I've got to get to the office." He stood and moved to the sink, rinsing out his cup and setting it on the counter. "Text me to let me know what you need from town for your trip and I'll pick it up. I'll be back around noon with some lunch and groceries for dinner. Give the kids a hug for me when they wake up."

"Sounds good. Say hi to your friend for me." Veronica laughed, a knowing smile lingering on her lips.

Liam waved and headed out the door to the patrol car. He drove across town and parked, hurrying to get inside.

He tossed his keys on the desk. "Good morning, everyone. Sorry I missed the briefing. Sergeant Peters, perhaps you'll catch me up."

"Must be nice to be late and not have the chief breathing down your neck," Mandy said, her tone causing him to recoil.

"I called in. So what are the highlights of the meeting," he asked again, as the others returned to work.

The rigid set of her shoulders and the careful way she avoided looking at him, sent warning signals through his brain. "Other than a couple of neighbors arguing about fence lines, it was a quiet night. And I've got a file to work on, so you'll have to ride solo today," she said, her icy voice giving him the chills.

Everyone stopped what they were doing and stared, the sudden silence deafening.

Liam frowned. "Surely the file can wait. I've got something I want to talk to you about," he said, hoping to move her past her bad mood.

"No, it can't wait," Mandy said, then she turned and marched out of the room, her boots clicking sharply against the floor.

All he'd done was leave her with Edith at the pizza parlor last night. Nothing that deserved the arctic treatment she was dishing out. Liam followed her into the copy room. "What's wrong?"

Mandy spun around and faced him, her eyes flashing with anger. "I think the better question is, what's right? Because it's certainly not you."

Liam shut the door for privacy, the click of the latch echoing in the small space. "What's that supposed to mean?"

"Where were you this morning?" she asked, her voice trembling with emotion. "Why are you late?"

"I've got houseguests. What about it? This isn't exactly a punch-in, punch-out job. Again, what's eating at you?" Liam asked, struggling to understand what was going on.

"I don't enjoy being played a fool. I saw you last night. In the park. The same woman and kids, I'm guessing, who spent the night with you. Looks like you've got a girlfriend you forgot to mention, Liam."

Understanding dawned, bringing him a surge of relief. "How is that playing you for a fool? And she's not a girlfriend. I told you a friend was in town, and I had to meet her." And you seemed fine with it at the time.

"She's important enough that you walked out on our date and you were kissing her. Yes, I saw that too."

Liam paused, a slight smile tugging at his lips as the pieces fell into place. "A date, huh? I like the sound of that, but with Edith there, I don't think it counts." Liam relaxed, realizing Mandy was jealous. And for no good reason. What he knew, now more than ever, was that she was coming to care for him as well. Today was a good day—or it would be once he cleared the air.

"A date with the both of us. Not me. Don't read anything into what I said And it doesn't change a thing. You were hugging and kissing your friend in the park. You're not the guy I thought you were." Mandy wasn't cutting him any slack, but then she didn't know what he knew.

Liam stalled telling her the truth, more than a little curious about her feelings toward him. "What kind of guy did you think I was, Mandy?" He took a step closer.

"That you were one of the nice guys. Against all odds, I liked you. A lot. Past tense." She huffed.

A nice guy. She liked me. All good to hear. "Veronica is my late partner's wife and those are their kids."

Mandy blanched, swallowing hard as she absorbed his comment. "And you were kissing her?"

"There was no kissing going on. Not the kind that counts the way you're thinking. We hugged, and I kissed her on the cheek. She's worried about some things and I've been like a big brother to her since Brock was killed. Someone keeps sending her letters that creep her out. The latest one is over the top and she was scared and came to me for safety."

Mandy relaxed, a shy smile back on her face. "Oh. I'm sorry. I guess I shouldn't have jumped to conclusions."

"No, you shouldn't. It's not good police work, but in this case, I'm glad you made the mistake."

"How's that? You're not making any sense," Mandy said, her brow furrowed.

Liam grinned. "Now I know you like me. And for the record, I like you too." He took another step closer.

Mandy shot a nervous glance at the door.

"Relax. No one can hear or see us in this room, and this is a private conversation."

"It changes nothing, Liam. You're my boss. Unless I quit. That's what Edith's husband did for them to be together."

Liam took a step forward. "Don't do that. I promise you'll regret it. This is your life, and I'm not here to mess it up." He closed the distance between them and took her hand.

"I don't think—"

Liam kissed her. Short and sweet. "Don't think."

The soft light in her eyes meant she got the message.

"Have dinner with me. Veronica and the kids are flying out early this evening and I'd love you to meet them first. By the way, she said to tell you hi."

Mandy looked confused. "But she doesn't know me."

"I told her about you. That's all she needed to hear. We could have dinner at my place after they've left. Away from prying eyes. It will give us a chance to get to know each other better."

Mandy smiled and nodded, finally giving in to what she really wanted. "Okay. If you're sure. But this could cause huge problems. I'm not sure what either of us wants in our life."

Liam shrugged. "I'm not so sure about that. So, it's a date. An actual date." He shot her a wink, then turned and left.

While out patrolling the quiet streets of Crossroads Creek, Liam decided it was a good time to call in a few favors. After coordinating with Chief Wilcox in Dallas, Liam had the go ahead to send Veronica's letter to the labs to check for fingerprints or any other identifying marks. His friend would check the letter without alerting anyone else about what he was working on or why. Liam hoped they had better luck this time since they would also add a handwriting analysis to the profile.

He called his buddy in Austin to expedite the files on Mandy's case to him. With Mandy back at the station, it would be easier to explain what he needed and why. He pulled over and parked in front of the diner.

Liam scrolled through his contacts and found Gerome Hanson, a detective at the Austin PD, and pressed the dial button.

"Hey Ben. It's been a while since I heard from you. You must want something," Gerome joked, though he was almost always right.

The two hadn't worked together for years and they didn't live close enough to hang out, so they drifted apart, other than work occasionally. "Sorry, but I've been caught up with work. And you guessed it, I need something. First, how's the wife and kids?"

"Doing great. Laura's pregnant again. This will be our fourth and last."

"That's what you said last time." Liam chuckled. "More power to you, buddy."

"Kids always seem to have just enough cute moments that make you think about babies again. It didn't take much for Laura to convince me. You know, it's high time you settled down, my friend. Start a family of your own."

"You're doing enough for the both of us and my job keeps me busy and all over the state," Liam teased, though for the first time, he wondered if his friend was right. About the settling down part. The kid part, not so much. Liam and his dad were never close, his dad too much of an authoritarian to cut his kid slack. It was also why his dad was Captain of the police department back then. Liam was worried he'd be the same taskmaster parent as his father. All he wanted was some fun times with his dad, times he never seemed to get. And never would.

"Where are you?" Gerome asked.

"Working a case so can't give out specifics. You know the drill."

"Sure do, after twelve years. What do you need? I'm on my way to pick up my oldest boy from school. Nurse's office called and they're sending him home with a runny nose and low-grade fever."

"That doesn't sound good," Liam said, glad it wasn't a problem he had to deal with.

"Kids are kids. They're sick all the time as every germ out there gets passed around at school. I'm used to it. So spill," Gerome said, getting to the point of the conversation.

"There's a divorced couple by the names of Mandy and John Roberts and there should be a kidnapping case filed on them from eight years ago. John's second wife's name is Tiffany Roberts. They are all from the Austin area and I'd like you to see what you can find on them. My boss will give you the authorization shortly, but I would love for you to put a rush on this for me."

"Anything specific you're after?" Gerome asked.

"Family ties. Criminal history. Photos. Job history. That sort of thing. And if you can email it as soon as possible, that would be great." He'd have to stop by the print shop in town to print the file, but it was better than breaking his cover location.

"I'll get right on it after I drop my boy off at the house. Give me about an hour, maybe a little more. Sounds like easy info to come by."

"Thanks. And give my best to Laura. Tell her I said congratulations...again." Liam teased.

"Thanks, man."

After hanging up, Liam headed to Courtney's Deli and grabbed a sandwich to go, preferring to sit in the car and think things through as he waited for the information from Gerome. True to his word, the email came through in a record time of forty-five minutes. He headed into the print shop and made a beeline for the self-help printer. After clicking several buttons, he attached the photos Gerome sent and then hit print.

Page after page of information came through. Several photos caught his attention, one more than others. Mandy looked the same, just younger. Long brown, curly hair, bright sapphire blue eyes, and smiling as she held her newborn daughter, her love reflected in the radiance of her expression.

Liam gathered up the documents and headed back to the patrol car. Once inside, he sifted through the information. He paused momentarily on the picture of John and Tiffany and their daughter. A happy, smiling family.

It was then he came across some startling news. John and Tiffany were hit by a drunk driver and died a few months ago. Their daughter, Sylvia Roberts, had been placed in a children's home with no mention of close family or distant relatives. And no one had come forward to claim the girl.

The police report of the accident had a special note that John Roberts, before he died, told paramedics to *Find Deedee. Sylvia. Find Deedee. Sylvia.* Child services were actively looking for a woman by the name of Deedee but had yet to find her.

Liam pondered the shocking news. Perhaps Deedee was a sister or an aunt. Long-lost friend. It was hard to say. The birth certificate listed her birthday as July fifteenth, meaning the girl would turn nine soon. He felt sorry for her being in a strange place and having no family. Surely, someone would adopt her once social services cleared her for adoption.

He dug deeper into Mandy's file and read about the kidnapping. The file seemed to miss a lot of information and the line of questioning and statements, amateurish at best. Rookie officer handling a kidnapping case seemed out of character. Liam pulled John's file and searched back until he found the kidnapping information. Sure enough, it read the same, but with some included statements by John accusing his wife, Mandy, of negligence. The file cited a sleeping medication overdose, but Mandy had denied the charge. Oddly enough, they dropped the matter. And two weeks later,

Mandy and John split up and were soon divorced. At no point did anyone question John, which was equally confusing as it would have been standard procedure to question both parties separately. The officer's name on the case, P.W. Williams.

Liam would love to question the officer, but he'd have to tread lightly. Maybe Gerome could get him some information on the guy.

Liam: Thanks for the great info. Exactly what I needed. Any chance you can tell me if P.W. Williams is still working at the Austin PD? And any other info you might have on him you think would interest me.

Gerome: I can. But it'll cost you. One free night of babysitting.

Liam: Consider it done. You might regret it, but I know I will. LOL.

Gerome: I'll hold you to it one day if you're ever in the area. As to PS Williams. Name is Phillip Williams, and he left the Austin PD three years ago. His wife was sick, and he couldn't keep up with job and home life, so he quit the force.

Liam: I see. Any chance you know if he's still in town? Where he's working now?

Gerome: Public records database shows him living in Wylie, TX.

That single piece of information was startling and way too much coincidence for Liam's liking.

Liam: Exactly what I needed to know. Thanks.

Gerome: Anytime. Don't be a stranger.

Chapter Thirteen

DRIVING TO BEN'S PLACE, Mandy's stomach fluttered with nerves After wrongly assuming Veronica was Liam's girlfriend, she would now meet both her and her children. *Lord, give me strength for whatever comes next.*

It warmed something deep inside her that Liam had told his friend about her, though she wondered what prompted the conversation. More than a little curious, she wondered what he said about them, because she herself wasn't entirely sure where they stood.

Liked? Definitely. Respected? Without question. Cared about, perhaps more than like? Yes, to all the above. But could she open herself up to love again? Over the past couple of weeks, Liam had settled in at the department, and everyone was finally beginning to relax and genuinely like him. His willingness to tackle any task, even as captain, was earning him the respect of the other officers.

Just like every other challenge in her life, Mandy forced her fears aside, ready to meet Liam's special friend. She pulled into the driveway and parked. Not even halfway to the house, he came out to meet her, a welcoming smile on his face.

"I'm so glad you joined us," Liam said, taking her by the hand and leading her to the porch.

"Thanks for the invite. I'm a little nervous, just saying," she admitted.

"Don't be. You'll love Veronica and the kids as much as I do when you get to know them."

Moments later, a tall, slender woman came out of the house, followed by a boy of about eight or nine. "This is Veronica, a very dear friend of mine, and her son, Ethan." He turned to Veronica. "And this is Mandy, my patrol partner at work."

Not a girlfriend, special friend, or even friend. Just partner. Maybe she'd read too much into his kisses and comments. "Nice to meet you, Veronica and Ethan," she said, holding out her hand in a friendly greeting. Veronica's hands were soft and well-manicured, unlike her own.

"Likewise. Liam has told me so much about you," Veronica said, grinning at Liam.

"Hopefully all good, considering we had a rough start." Mandy chuckled.

"Are you a cop too?" the boy asked, just as twin girls joined them.

Judging by their cute dimples and baby teeth smiles, they were probably around six. And totally adorable. "I am," Mandy said.

The boy's eyes lit up. "That's cool. We don't know any lady cops."

Mandy grinned. "Now you do."

One of the little girls yanked on her pant leg, her eyes clouded with concern. "Aren't you afraid of the bad guys?"

She leaned down, coming face to face with the child. "Not really. I've got the law on my side and some excellent fellow officers to back me up. We are all highly trained to do our jobs."

Veronica stepped forward. "Enough with all the career questions. Run inside and let the grownups talk." She shooed them all toward the door.

The children dashed inside. Mandy would bet they were playing video games and most likely preferred to continue but had been forced to stop what they were doing to come and meet her. Their mother was teaching them good manners.

They sat down in two oversized wicker chairs with thick green cushions.

"Ladies, I'll get us a couple of seltzer waters and be right back," Liam said, as he pulled open the door.

"Thanks," both women said in unison.

The minute the door closed, Veronica edged closer in her seat. "Liam's got a big heart, but he's kept it under wraps for the longest time. You're the first woman I've met that he's interested in. Be good to him, that's all I'm asking," she urged, keeping her voice low and soft.

Mandy shook her head, surprised by not only Veronica's comment, but at just how personal it was coming from a virtual stranger. "You've got this all wrong. We're just friends."

Veronica grinned. "Baloney. I see the way you look at each other. So, if you're in denial, you're only kidding yourself. Face it, girl, you like him. A lot."

Was the woman psychic, or had Mandy become that transparent with her feelings? "Our jobs make anything between us a problem."

Veronica reached out and took her hand, yet again surprising Mandy. "Then one of you should change jobs. Love is so much bigger than work. And love, when you find it, is golden. And it can be fleeting. It's important to grab on to happiness when you find it." Her voice broke as her eyes misted.

It was like suddenly having a new best friend, something that didn't come easy to Mandy. Though Veronica was hard to dislike at this point. "I'm sorry about your husband. Liam explained, your *umm*, relationship with him. As for Liam and me, it's all so new. And to be honest, I do care about him. A lot, just like you already know. It's just an enormous leap to use the word love. I don't have a great track record."

Veronica took both of Mandy's hands in hers. "Don't complicate it. Let your heart feel. Pray about it. God can do wonders in your life if you let him. I had my wonderful life, and now I focus on the kids Brock and I created together when he was alive."

The simple faith in Veronica's words touched something deep inside Mandy. Perhaps it was time to give Liam and love a chance. The door opened, cutting off any chance of a reply or further conversation on the current subject.

The three of them stayed on the front porch talking like old friends Veronica regaling her with stories about Liam, much to his chagrin. She was a sweetheart, and Mandy regretted ever accusing Liam there was anything between them. The woman was very much still in love with Brock, and in a way, it touched her deeply to see such a great love between two people that even death couldn't end. But it also made her heart ache for Veronica's pain.

An hour later, Veronica stood. "It's time I got a move on. We're all packed and the car is loaded, but I've got to get the kids in the car and head for the airport."

"Are you sure you don't want me to drive you? It's not a problem and you know it," Liam said.

Veronica shook her head. "No, no. It's easier this way for everyone. I'm going to call a friend to get my car. That way, I don't rack up the parking bill. Maybe you could pick us up in Dallas when we return in a couple of weeks."

"Sounds like a plan. You can count on me being there, and I already have all your flight information," Liam added.

Veronica disappeared inside.

Liam turned back to Mandy. "Hope you're okay with spaghetti for dinner?"

"I love spaghetti. It's messy, but I'm game." Mandy laughed.

"Good. I don't cook much, but I typically can't mess up something so basic. Need to make a good first impression on you," he teased. "We're way past first impressions and yours was a doozy."

The door opened and Veronica and the kids came out on the porch, each one sporting a backpack with what Mandy assumed was plane activities.

"It's been wonderful to meet you, Mandy. Just remember what we talked about." Veronica grinned, pulling her in for a hug.

"I enjoyed meeting you, too. I'll think it over," Mandy said, knowing it was true.

Liam and the kids and Veronica hugged and said their goodbyes, and then, just like that, she was alone with Liam.

"What did you and Veronica talk about? Her comment has made me curious," Liam asked.

"Oh, nothing much. Just girl talk." She wasn't about to share that conversation, especially when she wasn't sure what to do about it. But her heart felt lighter than it had in years. Mandy was glad she had said yes to dinner, as this would be the first real chance for them to spend quality time together. Alone.

The aroma of garlic and tomatoes filled the kitchen as Liam stirred the sauce. "I warned you this is about the extent of my culinary skills," he said, offering her a tentative smile.

"It smells wonderful," Mandy said, leaning against the counter. The homey scene stirred something in her heart—how long had it been since she had shared a simple meal with someone she cared about?

"Here, taste this." Liam held out the wooden spoon, his other hand cupped beneath to catch any drips.

She leaned forward, their eyes meeting as she tasted the sauce. "*Mmmm.* Perfect amount of oregano."

"You've got a little..." Liam gestured to her cheek, then reached out to gently wipe away a spot of sauce with his thumb. The tender gesture turned into a soft caress, and Mandy's breath caught as he leaned in to kiss her.

The kiss was sweet and unhurried, filled with promise. When they separated, Mandy smiled despite the complications this attraction presented. "We probably shouldn't be doing this," she murmured, though she made no move to step away. "It's against department protocol." Something she mentioned repeatedly, but so far, had little effect on her decisions.

Liam's eyes held both warmth and concern. "I know. I'll figure something out. I enjoy being with you, Mandy. You help me understand things about my past I've been running from for too long."

"I feel the connection, too," she admitted. The truth of it settled in her heart but not her head. "But the department—"

"One step at a time," he said squeezing her hand. "Right now, let's just enjoy dinner before the pasta turns to mush."

"I'll be right back. Make yourself comfortable," Liam said after they'd cleaned and put away the dishes and leftovers.

The warmth from their shared meal lingered as Mandy wandered around the living room, struck by how little Liam seemed to have settled in the place. There were no family photos hanging on the walls, or personal effects one could call his. The old furniture had seen better days and must have come with the rental. The wooden floors, worn from decades of use, creaked beneath her feet. Paint peeled from the walls in a few places. It was a wonder he was still living here and hadn't found a permanent place to stay yet. Another piece of the Liam puzzle that just didn't seem to fit.

Come to think of it, she couldn't recall that he was even looking. The place had a quaint rustic charm, but definitely needed some tender loving care. Drawn to the fireplace, she inspected the one portrait she'd noticed in the room, hanging over the mantel. Mandy realized it was the same house, just in sepia tones that reflected the home in its glory days. A time when the ranch house was well cared for.

Her gaze drifted to the initials carved on the mantel. BC. This was the old Calhoun place, but she didn't have a clue about their names, having only moved here four years ago. She continued to inspect the room, moving to a desk in the corner, trying to learn more about Liam and soaking up his quiet presence in the house. Scattered books and files were strewn across the surface. Mandy stacked the books to help him get organized. It was then she spotted a file sticking out from under one book. A file with her name on the tab.

Mandy's heart stuttered as she lifted the file with trembling fingers. The photo clipped to the top stopped her cold—it was of her, years younger, smiling beside John. The image was of a woman who still believed in love and happily-ever-after. That woman didn't exist anymore.

She opened the folder to reveal a background check, and her personnel files from the Austin PD and Crossroads Creek PD—her entire career as a police officer. Her stomach clenched as she flipped through the pages, each one feeling like another invasion of her personal life. A total betrayal by the man she cared for and trusted. Clearly, her instincts had been all wrong.

Why would Liam have all this information on her? The folder was thick, as though it had her entire life history in it. For a guy just claiming he was getting to know the staff, he had gone way beyond the call of duty with this file. She inspected the rest of his desk and couldn't find files on anyone else from the department, which laid a lie to his claim about checking up on everyone. It would seem his review was focused mostly on her. The question was, *why*? Because none of this made any sense, and unless he was a dirty cop, it stood to reason he went through a lot of channels to get this information, and that means he had to have probable cause.

Liam came back into the room. "Do you want to watch a—"

"What are you doing with a file on me?" Mandy demanded, coming to her feet and shaking the folder at him.

Liam paled, his eyes on the file in her hand. "Calm down. I'm just doing background checks and getting to know everyone and what makes them tick. It's routine for a new boss coming in cold."

Mandy fought to keep control of her anger. He betrayed her trust and deserved to know why. "Except it's only my file you seem to have, and you have way more than a background check. Are you investigating me for something?"

He shook his head and moved closer, the lines of tension on his forehead more like deep ravines. "No, it's not what you think."

Mandy brushed away the tears running down her face. "Then what is it, Liam? You have some explaining to do and I demand answers," she said, clutching the file to her chest.

Liam let out a deep sigh. 'I'd rather not discuss this. Actually, I can t discuss this. Whichever you prefer, they both apply. Just trust me when I say it's not what you think. I need you to give me the benefit of the doubt. Please," he added.

Years of police training taught her to ferret out liars, and Mandy would bet her entire career Liam was lying to her face. "And why would I do that? Because you've kissed me a few times? That hardly calls for blind trust. I'm leaving."

"Mandy, wait. Please understand, I'm just not at liberty to discuss this. You know the routine as well as I do." He raked a hand through his hair, his anguished expression almost giving her reason to doubt.

Then it hit her what he said. "Not at liberty to discuss. As in—the case. So, you are investigating me." This newest piece of information cut even deeper. "I demand to know what for? I have done nothing wrong. Oh, no." Her voice broke. "Please don't tell me this is related to what I shared with you about the kidnapping. Let me guess, you think I had something to do with my daughter's disappearance, or that I was an unfit parent." The old guilt and pain surfaced, threatening to consume her. If he had the file, he also knew about the sleeping medication they said she took. Though they probably never recorded her side of the conversation when she revealed she had not taken anything that night. She was so tired she didn't need medication. How could he do this to her? She had confided in him, and this is where it landed her.

Under investigation.

Liam paled. "No, Mandy, no. You've got it all wrong. I never said I was investigating you, and that's a resounding no to both of your charges."

Mandy tossed the file on his desk. "It doesn't matter. We both know this was a mistake." She marched out the door, letting it slam behind her. Mandy didn't know what game he was playing, but she intended to find out.

With trembling fingers, Mandy hit the speed dial button for Chief Jackson.

"What's up, Sergeant Peters?"

"There's a lot going on behind the scenes at the office and I want to know what it is? Why is Captain Carter investigating me?" she demanded, the words coming out in a rush.

"Calm down. It's not what you think. He's not investigating you, I promise."

Why did they all keep telling her it wasn't what she thought? The coined phrase irked her to no end. Or was it that the chief didn't know the full extent of what Liam was up to, either? "Then what is he doing with a file thick enough to hold my entire life's history at his house? Did you authorize a subpoena for this information?"

"Why were you at his house?" Chief Jackson asked, skipping her questions, and zeroing in on what he considered a more important piece of information.

"It was dinner with a friend, which shouldn't pose a problem for anyone. Or that's all it was until I found out he's up to something and I'm deeply involved without even knowing why. It's a mistake I won't be repeating. I don't think Captain Carter is who he says he is. Why did you hire him? Where did he really come from? And what's his purpose here?" Mandy fired off the questions she wanted answered, and she was tired of getting the runaround.

"Captain Carter is just doing his job, Mandy. Let it go. That's an order." The evasion in his tone only confirmed her suspicions, and she was more convinced than ever he knew the truth.

"I quit," Mandy snapped.

"I wish you wouldn't. You are good at your job, and you promised me another week to sort things out."

"Finding that file and being kept in the dark about what's going on changes everything. I'm going to apply for a new job. Are you forgetting that recently you planned to promote me to captain? That should entitle me to some information, don't you think? Or is it that you don't trust me?" she pressed, hoping to convince him to bring her into the inner loop of information. It did, after all, concern her somehow.

The chief let out a heavy sigh. "Okay. You're right, something is going on. But I'm not at liberty to discuss the situation. Can you just trust me on this a little longer? Please."

His confirmation brought no satisfaction. The fact the chief was begging her to stick around made her feel somewhat better. Like her entire world wasn't about to fall apart and she'd end up in court. Or worse, in prison. "I'll stay for the rest of the week because I made a promise, but I'm not that man's partner anymore. Put Officer Smith with him."

"No problem. Consider it done," the chief said, without so much as a hint of objection.

"And I'm still leaving the CCPD." She huffed. "I don't like being kept in the dark about anything going on in this department. Consider my notice effective when I find a new job." It was for the best, as she knew there would never be room for two captains on such a small force. It was short-sighted to think he could ever fix the situation to her liking.

"Mandy, listen to me. I'm going to go out on a limb here and I pray you don't press me for more information or relay what I'm about to tell you to anyone. It could get both of us in a lot of trouble."

She jerked the wheel to the side of the road. "I'm listening, and you have my word." Finally, the truth.

"Captain Carter is working undercover on a case. That's all you need to know."

The revelation hit her square in the chest. It wasn't the whole story, but it was a start. "How does it involve me?"

"I can't answer that, but you're not being investigated for any wrong doing. Trust me on this."

Mandy let out a deep breath. She believed the chief about not being investigated, but that only opened up more painful questions. Then who kissed her? Who had made her believe in love again? And exactly who was he?

Because one thing was for certain, he wasn't Liam Carter.

Chapter Fourteen

♥

THE SUN BLINDED LIAM as he drove to work and he lowered the visor. He wasn't looking forward to today, steeling himself against Mandy's outrage. The memory of her hurt expression twisted like a knife in the gut. If she knew the whole truth, she would be even more furious and there was no telling what to expect.

The text Chief Jackson sent him didn't help matters. Mandy now knew he was working undercover, but not why, and she was refusing to work with him. The mounting complications weighed heavily on his mind. There would be a lot of raised eyebrows and questions at the turn of events with a switch in partners, and yet there would be no answers forthcoming. That would make the others more uncomfortable, and any officer good at his job would start trying to find the answers on their own.

The past couple of weeks in Crossroads Creek had changed Liam in ways he hadn't expected, bringing him closer to a faith he had long ago abandoned. He had Mandy to thank for opening his eyes, though talking to him was the last thing she wanted now.

Perhaps it was better this way. There were too many obstacles for any genuine relationship with Mandy, and it would have been an uphill battle all the way, trying to figure out how to make it work. In less than a week, he'd be back in Dallas—maybe even sooner if some of the new leads he got on the case panned out. Then it was on to the next case.

Liam entered the office amidst curious glances and stares. "Morning, Mandy," he said, stopping at her desk, knowing he had to break the ice sometime. "The patrol car is all yours as I've got some paperwork to handle in the office today," he said, tossing the keys on her desk, hoping to sidestep any conversation about last night.

Mandy was tight-lipped and gave no response, other than a curt nod that spoke volumes. The temperature in the room just dropped ten degrees with her icy stare.

Liam headed for his desk. He intended to go over all the details of the kidnapping case in Wylie, and the other eight kidnappings over the past eight years, which now included Mandy's daughter's kidnapping. There had to be a connection, and it was his job to figure it out, even though her case wasn't part of the original linked cases. In some ways, it made her case all that much more important, hoping it would hold some answers they had yet to figure out.

Hours later, he stretched, rubbing the back of his neck. Off to the side of his desk, he noticed the folders he had on the Wylie and Fontana police departments. Liam perused the documents, citing the names and time on the force. Something made him go back over the list. A feeling he was missing an important piece of information.

Nothing.

Liam returned to look over the Robert's kidnapping file. PS Williams was the case officer who handled the shoddy report. He jotted down the name on a sheet of paper and added the date of the report. Officer Phillip Williams handled another one of the cases five years ago, and Liam jotted down that date as well.

Williams. He could have sworn he saw that name at least three times. One by one he went through the cases again, and on the last one, he found what he was looking for. Scott Williams' name jumped out from the Wylie kidnapping paperwork, though it was a poorly documented case report. Not only that, but the status of the case had been updated recently as closed, much to Liam's surprise. It meant no one was investigating it. Had the child been found?

And why wasn't he informed of these developments?

PS Williams. Phillip Williams. Scott Williams. What were the chances it was a total coincidence in names? His pulse raced, intuition kicking in like a punch to the gut. Liam knew he was on to something big. *Or wishful thinking.* Time to do a little digging on Officer Williams of the Wylie PD. He headed for Chief Jackson's office, intent on sharing his findings in order to get a subpoena for the officer's full professional and personal records.

He rapped sharply on the door and headed inside. Taking a seat, Liam waited for the chief to hang up the phone.

"What's up, Captain Carter? Hopefully nothing to do with Officer Peters as I've about had it up to here," he said, his hand level with his chest, "in trying to keep her from leaving the department while you dance around the county doing your investigation."

"It does involve Officer Peters, but not between her and I. There's a possible new lead in the cases. It could be the break law en-forcement has needed, but I'll need a sub-poena to investigate my hunch any further," he said, keeping his voice low.

"Better be more than a hunch if you ex-pect a subpoena," the chief said, tossing his glasses on the table and giving Liam his undivided attention.

"You know I can get one from Chief Wilcox, but going through you would be quicker, so I'm hoping you'll push this through. We can't afford to have any slip ups because if I'm right and this guy gets wind of anything coming down his way, he'll be gone in a split second." Not only that, but Liam was on a deadline with Mandy. What he needed was solid proof.

"I still have to have a valid reason and proof of probable cause."

"What if I told you that three of the now nine cases were handled by an officer named Williams? Officer PS Williams, Officer Phillip Williams, and Officer Scott Williams. Two of these cases were in Austin, and the last one right here in Wylie."

The chief's chair creaked as he sat up straighter. "An officer? I don't believe it. I pray you're wrong about him. Scott Williams is a nice enough guy and I would have never suspected him. Guy just lost his wife to cancer. I thought there were eight cases. How is it nine now?"

"Officer Mandy Peters was married to John Roberts eight years ago, before she became a police officer. Her daughter was kidnapped two years before we started tracking the cases and it was missed as being the same MO. The report details weren't all listed on the computer file and it was an infant that was kidnapped so it wasn't linked."

Chief Jackson pushed to his feet and started pacing the office. "This is unbelievable. How did I not know this?"

"She doesn't talk about it, and it happened before she became a police officer, so it's not a part of her personnel records at either location she's worked. Anyway, this PS Williams did some pretty shoddy work on the case and the paperwork. And Scott Williams recently closed the case on the Wylie kidnapping, but there's no record if the child was even found. Something's very wrong here."

"And this is why you have a huge file on Mandy? A file I know nothing about. I take it she doesn't know what you're actually investigating, or else I would think she would be all over this discovery."

Liam's conscience pricked at him. "No, she doesn't know, and I don't want her to find out. Not yet, anyway." Liam relayed the story about Mandy and John Roberts, and then John and his second wife, Tiffany. He intentionally left out the parts about the police questioning Mandy's abilities as a mother and the sleeping medication, or the fact she was listed initially as a suspect in her daughter's disappearance. "It's quite the coincidence John and Tiffany had a daughter together with a birthday ten days later than John and Mandy's daughter's birthday. Either both women were pregnant, and John was cheating on Mandy, or something even more sinister was going on. I aim to find out which. The kicker is, John and Tiffany died about three months ago and their daughter, Sylvia, is at a children's home. Social services are looking for a Deedee, some woman they guess might be distantly related, but so far, no luck. It was something John said on his deathbed at the scene of the accident linking Sylvia, his daughter, and this Deedee woman."

Movement caught his eye and Liam glanced around the office through the glass, shocked to see Mandy just outside the chief's office. His heart dropped to his stomach, her stricken look as she stood frozen, chilling him to the core. He got up and closed the door, kicking himself for not doing it beforehand. Luckily, she would have had a hard time making out the conversation.

"Sir, it's always possible John was involved in the kidnapping of his own daughter. If so, that would mean there's a chance this Sylvia girl might be Mandy's daughter. It's a long shot, but any possibility needs to be investigated. I want to do everything in my power to find out, but there is no way I want to put Mandy through the heartache if I'm wrong."

The chief nodded, understanding dawning in his wrinkled features. "Good point, and I trust your instincts. You were right—this could be a huge break. Nice work, Captain Carter. On another note, you and Officer Peters were getting quite chummy before last night's fiasco. You know that's not allowed while you are working on my staff."

Liam understood the warning. "Officer Peters is an excellent police officer, and we agree on most things, which helped us to become friends." *Kissing friends*, but that, too, had ended.

"Nothing else?" the chief pressed.

He shook his head, needing to dispel the notion, not wanting to put a mark on Mandy's stellar reputation with the department. "You know I'm leaving soon. Headed back to Dallas, so even if I wanted here be, it's not possible. Though being fair, I've enjoyed my time here in Crossroads Creek and getting to know people."

"The place grows on you. I can't imagine you leaving the first time, much less the second."

A familiar ached squeezed his chest, but he wasn't prepared to discuss his personal life. "It's a long story. Sir, about the subpoena?"

"I'll have it on your desk within the hour. What do you want it to include?"

"All of Officer Williams personnel files from all the police departments he has worked for, including disciplinary actions. I'd also like bank records for the past eight years and credit information, and any other financial records. The standard places to look for a problem as a starting point."

"Consider it done," the chief said, picking up the phone and signaling their conversation was over.

***

Mandy had noticed the chief and Liam talking privately, and her curiosity went into overdrive. She had walked down the hall that took her right past the chief's office, hoping to catch bits and pieces of conversation, coffee mug in hand as a cover. What she hadn't expected was to hear her name. Her nickname.

Looking for a Deedee. She had stood there frozen, unable to grasp the significance. No one except her ex-husband knew the nickname. She had wanted to barge into the office and demand information, but she also knew they would clam up on her. It appeared her daughter's kidnapping was a part of Liam's investigation. The question was, why? Were they trying to tie her to the kidnapping? Was she a suspect again? Her legs had felt like lead, but she forced herself to continue down the hall to the coffee room after Liam closed the door.

She fought to regain control as her head continued spinning with possibilities like a tropical summer storm. None of them good, and all of them centered on Liam's arrival in Crossroads Creek. His lack of trust, faith, and the irony of it all were mind-boggling. Not to mention the Chief Jackson had just assured Mandy of his trust in her abilities.

Except it would seem Liam was bending the chief's ear, and it was all about her. Was everything she had carefully organized in her life about to come tumbling down around her head?

Trust in the Lord with all your heart.

Mandy was leaving the CCPD soon anyway. Inwardly seething, she returned to her desk. Gathering up her belongings into a box, she then typed a resignation letter and put Chief Jackson's name on the front. She propped it up against her desk phone and dropped the patrol car keys next to it.

They were such good detectives, let them figure out she wasn't coming back.

Chapter Fifteen

♥

AFTER LEAVING THE CHIEF'S office, Liam needed to talk to Mandy. Her expression when she stood frozen, gaping at him, left him in a quandary. She might not want to like him, but he needed to somehow patch things up. Her desk was empty, and at first he thought she might have gone out on patrol, but when he noticed the keys and envelope, he knew something was terribly wrong.

Liam delivered the letter to Chief Jackson, but in his gut he knew what the contents would be.

Chief Jackson read the letter and tossed it on his desk. "She up and quit. So, I guess our time was up for explanations," he said, running a hand through his hair as though losing a trusted employee pained him. "Fix this, Captain Carter. Now."

Liam wasn't sure what he could do. "But sir..."

"No. Get her back. The department can't afford to lose her," Chief Jackson said, suddenly looking older than his fifty-eight years.

He nodded. "I'll think of something. Or at least try. I promise." Liam left the office, not even remotely knowing what to say or do. Mandy had good reason to leave, given what was going on. And of course, being left in the dark didn't help matters. But it was for her own protection, not that she knew or understood his reasoning. Liam wanted nothing more than to tell her, but what if he was wrong? The effect on Mandy would be devastating, and there was no way he would put her through the emotional upheaval.

Unless he was right.

Liam prayed over what to do, which came as a total surprise. Something else Mandy was responsible for in his life. Getting him to open up to faith and love again. Throughout her entire ordeal, and the years after, she trusted in God and her faith to pull through the bad days. Something he had failed to do. And of the two of them, she had been more settled, more at peace with the past.

One never forgets a painful memory, but one could live again and make a new life. Something Liam was coming to understand. He'd run from Crossroads Creek, and yet now he was back, and it was as though he had never left. Memories floated through the old house, some good, some bad. But they were his life. This was the closest he had felt to his parents and sister since they died. It hurt. Deeply hurt. But shutting them out of his life had done no good.

He prayed he was right about Sylvia Roberts. Unfortunately, it would bring home a whole new depth of emotions and trauma for Mandy to accept her ex-husband's deception and level of involvement. She might never recover from such a blow, which would be a travesty because Mandy was made for love, peace, and family. But if he was right, Mandy's prayer would be answered, and she'd have her daughter back. A bigger blessing to see her through the hard truth.

Liam pulled into Mandy's driveway, preparing himself for the expected onslaught of her anger. He wouldn't be here now if it weren't for the chief's special demand, hoping to change her mind. What could he do or say more than he already had without revealing the truth? He would try, but he wasn't expecting a miracle. He knocked at her front door, the sound matching his rapid heartbeat.

Frieda's excited barking from inside was followed by the sound of footsteps on the tile floor and the sound of a lock turning.

Mandy stood there, glaring at him. "What do you want?" she snapped. "I'm in no mood to talk to the likes of you, Mr. Undercover Investigator."

He deserved her comment and then some. "Please, just a few minutes of your time. The chief sent me to talk to you."

She hesitated, but surprisingly, joined him on the porch, letting Frieda run and play in the yard. Mandy looked up at the blue sky, remained silent, and then visibly relaxed. It was clear she'd been praying for peace. He would have to try that sometime because it certainly seemed to work for her.

"What do you want?" she asked again.

"The chief has refused your request." Liam pulled her resignation letter from his pocket and tried to hand it to her, but she didn't move a muscle.

Hands on hips, she glared at him. "Are you, or are you not, investigating me?"

"Mandy, you know—"

"What I know is that someone better start talking. I'll call the DA's office if I have to. You can't investigate me without probable cause."

Liam shook his head. "I've already explained I'm not investigating you—per se." This was the tricky part as he tried to balance how much to reveal.

"Then what or who are you investigating, and how did you find out about my nickname? No one knows it, except my ex-husband, that is."

Liam staggered back as if physically struck, the revelation stealing his breath. "Your nickname? I'm confused."

"When I was walking by the office today, I heard you mention the name Deedee. I know it's not a coincidence."

"You're Deedee?" he asked, reconfirming he was hearing this correctly. The wicker chair creaked under his weight as Liam collapsed into it, his mind racing to process this game-changing piece of information.

"Yes, that's what I'm trying to tell you. It was a nickname John used to call me. But how is it you didn't know it was me? Unless this is all an act."

"No act. Let me think about this for a moment." His heart hammered in his chest. If

Mandy was Deedee and her name was on John's dying lips with his daughter's name, was the man trying to fix a wrong and make sure Sylvia and her mother were reunited? What if John simply wanted a parent figure for his daughter, knowing he was going to die? A significant difference with incredibly different outcomes. The pieces of the puzzle were shifting, forming a new and startling picture. Liam was on the verge of telling Mandy, but he could still be wrong.

He needed concrete proof before he could share this information with Mandy, but in his heart he already knew the answer. He was almost positive they would discover Sylvia was her daughter, and that John had arranged for their daughter to be kidnapped. It all made sense now.

The question was, why? And who helped him pull it off? John and Tiffany couldn't be charged anymore with the crime, but whoever helped them would pay dearly.

"Where did you hear my nickname, Liam?" she persisted.

He shook his head, knowing he had to keep this under wraps for now. "I can't say. Not yet. Trust me on this."

"I'm tired of all the secrecy. For the last time, what is going on?" she demanded.

Liam needed more time. He stood and took her hand in his, though she tried to pull away. "Give me forty-eight hours and I should be able to answer all your questions." He prayed it was enough time, and he wouldn't sleep until he figured this out.

Mandy seemed to consider his words. She visibly relaxed. "Fine. Forty-eight hours and no more. I'll hold you to your promise, Captain Carter," she said, pulling her hand from his and taking a step back.

"Ben Calhoun."

"What?" she asked, her brow scrunched in confusion.

"That's my real name." Telling a piece of the truth was like a weight off his shoulders.

He sensed a deep need for her to know his name and to hear his name on her lips. Not his pseudo character.

"Calhoun? As in—"

"Yes. That's my ranch where I'm living. Please keep this to yourself for the time being, as I don't want to jeopardize the investigation."

A flicker of understanding softened her expression, and she nodded. "Thanks for trusting me with at least this much of the truth, Ben," she said, trying his name out.

"I would trust you with it all if I thought I knew the outcome of my findings. It's as much for you as it is for the investigation."

"I just wish I understood. Forty-eight hours and I expect an explanation."

"Clock's ticking." Liam managed a small smile before turning to leave, each step away from her harder than the last. Freida chased after him, but the puppy ran back to Mandy when she called him.

Smart dog.

Liam still couldn't believe Mandy was Deedee, the woman the state had been trying to track down. For Mandy, everything might turn up roses. Getting her daughter back after all these years would be a miracle, and as an added blessing, she would finally get the promotion she deserved. He, on the other hand, would be back in Dallas. Missing Mandy, but where he belonged, knowing she would never trust him again. Though his heart would forever remain in Crossroads Creek, he feared.

It was late, and he was tired, but he poured himself another cup of coffee, the bitter taste of the old brew keeping him awake. He had gone over and over each of the cases and was reviewing all the files on Officer Williams. Leaning back in his chair, he reviewed the notes he'd jotted down and then went through eight years of bank statements, starting with the oldest one. The numbers swam before his tired eyes until he spotted a large cash deposit of fifty grand. Heck of a bonus for a police officer. Liam circled the date and the amount and continued to scan the statement. A cash payment of roughly forty-eight thousand dollars was made to CTF. A quick search on the internet revealed it was the Cancer Treatment Facility.

Liam remembered Mandy and the chief mentioning Officer William's wife recently died of cancer. So where did the money come from? He jotted down the dates and the amounts and continued scanning the documents.

Almost three years later, another cash deposit was made. This one for a hundred thousand dollars. And a corresponding payment to CTF for sixty-five thousand dollars. He wrote down the information, putting a star next to both entries. It wasn't long after this, Officer Williams moved to Wylie. Documents showed he bought his house from the proceeds of the sale of his home in Austin, with some to spare, giving him a tidy little nest egg. Though his account continued to dwindle with payments to CTF. There was an injection of capital when he took out an equity loan on his house. But eventually, that money was also gone. Either William's family didn't have good insurance, or they had stopped paying it, because the medical bills were astronomical.

And then Liam saw something that made his head spin, and his pulse quicken. Another entry. Two months ago, there was a deposit for fifty-five thousand dollars, along with another payment to CTF. And the records show Phillip Williams was behind on his equity loan payments, a debt secured by his home. Two months ago, another child was kidnapped. This time in Wylie. His stomach churned as the implications sank in. Way too much coincidence. Liam had found motive, means, and proof that Officer Williams was involved. The dates of every large deposit transaction except the mortgage loan coincided within two weeks of three of the kidnappings, all cases Williams handled. This was more than a smoking gun. Between shoddy paperwork, early case closings, and lump sum deposits, they had enough to serve an arrest warrant to bring Officer Williams in for questioning.

Hopefully, Phillip cooperated. It could very well be the break they needed to put an end to the kidnapping ring in Texas. And maybe, if they were lucky, they could start tracking down some of the children with his help. A prayer of gratitude rose in his heart as he realized the first of the three cases Phillip was involved with would already have a happy ending because he knew where to find the child.

The children's home just outside of Austin.

Chapter Sixteen

♥

OFFICER PHILLIP WILLIAMS JUMPED to his feet when Liam entered the interrogation room to question him, the bright lights casting dark shadows across his face. Tension crackled in the air.

"I'm guessing you're the new officer in town that's irritating some of us that have been around for a while. I don't know what game you're playing, bringing me in like I'm some sort of criminal, and I demand an explanation," His indignation echoed off the bare walls of the room.

The metal chair scraped against the floor as Liam sat down at the end of the table with deliberate calm. "Sit down, Phillip. You'll get all the explanations you need, though you might not want to hear them. Ever heard the expression, three strikes and you're out? This last kidnapping case was your third strike, and you've been implicated beyond a doubt. Time to pay the piper."

A nervous tick pounded away at the side of Phillip's temple, the man's hands folded in front of him, but the bloodless fingers were a telltale sign of his stress level. "Just because I was the officer handling the kidnapping case does not make me in any way culpable," he snapped, his gaze darting around the room like a cornered animal.

Liam leaned forward. "Like I said, it's not one case—it's three," he said, his voice steady and determined. "And after some extensive digging into your background since the kidnappings began, there's enough evidence to put you behind bars. Three cases you've handled. Three cases you did a sloppy job on the report. Three times you received a large sum of money to pay CTF that corresponds to a time frame two weeks prior to the kidnapping cases you handled. Two in Austin and the most recent one in Wylie. You've got a lot of questions to answer Phillip Scott Williams," Liam added. His voice hardened on the last words.

Phillip blanched, though he struggled to keep his composure. Liam knew he had him dead to rights. It was just getting him to talk about it.

"Do you want to tell me what really happened and maybe I can put in a good word with the DA for you? Or do we let them have a field day and you sit behind bars waiting out a trial? Because there's no way you're walking away from this or out of here. There's just too much connecting the dots. There's only so much room for coincidence, and these are no coincidences." The weight of every stolen child's fate rested on him. A dirty cop was the worst of the worst, abusing their power for harm. There was a lot they still needed to know about how the ring operated and who was behind setting the kidnappings up. Liam was determined to put an end to the kidnapping ring. They needed Phillip Williams to help them make that happen.

"You can't prove I had anything to do with it," Phillip said, though not nearly as forcefully as before. He was weakening in his resolve to deny all charges.

Liam shook his head. "That's where you're wrong. Good luck trying to explain away those large deposits on your salary. Cash deposits at that."

Phillip shifted uncomfortably in his seat. "I need a lawyer. I'm not saying another word without one."

He fully expected Phillip to play the attorney card, though he was surprised it took him this long. "Suit yourself. It's your funeral. Or should I say prison cell? Not always a great place for a police officer to be when you're on the inside looking out."

Phillip swallowed hard and seemed to ponder his words for an extra moment. "I'll be out in no time. You should watch your back for a defamation of character lawsuit," he snapped. The false bravado in Phillip's voice highlighted his desperation.

Liam stood. "You and I both know those were empty threats. So, I'll ask you again, do you want to cooperate? Or shall we file formal charges against you for three counts of kidnapping?" He started for the door to make good on his claim.

"I didn't kidnap anybody. You can't charge me for something I didn't do. I had nothing to do with the kidnappings, I swear." Phillip wiped the sweat off his brow.

Liam made his way back to the table, putting his hands, palms flat to support him as he leaned close. "Maybe not, but as an accessory to kidnapping and for altering police reports, there are some heavy penalties, and you will definitely do prison time. Lots of it."

Phillip shook, head in hands, his shoulder slumped. Resignation was written in every muscle of his body. "Fine. I'll tell you what you want to know."

He read Phillip his Miranda rights. "This conversation will be recorded, and you understand you're waiving your right to have an attorney present? And for the record, my name is Texas Ranger Ben Calhoun."

Phillip's mouth dropped wide open. "I should have known you weren't some rookie cop who landed a cushy job. I'm toast. And yes, I understand my rights. I want to go on record and swear I kidnapped no one or had anything directly to do with criminals who were."

"Tell me what happened?" Ben prompted, relieved to let go of the alias.

"My wife was sick. Nobody seems to understand that. How was I to make payments to keep her alive? I loved my wife, and I was willing to do anything to keep her alive. Is that such a bad thing? I only altered records on those three cases because I knew the child would be well cared for. I swear I would never want a child to suffer." His words were muffled, but Ben understood every one of them.

Anger surged through Ben's veins. "So, you're a criminal with a heart. Is that what you're saying? And you think it's okay to hurt the parents and rip a child from their parents' arms? You say you loved your wife, but would she have loved what you did to help her?" The entire conversation was being recorded, and they just had an admission of guilt for altering the records. Phillip would spend a lot of time in prison for his misguided efforts to save his wife.

Phillip shook his head. "She never knew. Honestly, the first two times were just to keep her treatments going. And she was doing better for a time. We moved to Wylie, and then the cancer came back. The mortgage company didn't care—they wanted to just take our house. I did what I had to do to keep my wife alive and make her last months the best I could for her. She died shortly before the mortgage company started foreclosure proceedings."

"Save the sob story for the jury. Wrongdoings for a good cause are still wrongdoings."

Ben couldn't let the story steer him off course, though compassion seeped into his brain for the man in front of him.

"I know. I know. Don't think this hasn't consumed me. It's probably good it's over," Phillip said, defeat echoed in every word he spoke.

"If it has consumed you and you have any sense of right and wrong, then do the right thing and help us put a stop to this kidnapping ring. Help us find any of the kids if you can," Ben added, trying to keep a calm he wasn't feeling.

"My life is over, so I guess it doesn't matter anyway. What do you want to know?"

Ben's heart hammered in his chest as they neared one of the critical moments in Phillip's admission. "Let's start with Mandy and John Roberts eight years ago. Their one-week-old infant was kidnapped from their home. This was one of your cases, and I'm sure you remember what happened."

"And if I tell you all this, you're going to aim for some leniency and compassion in the sentencing, right?"

Ben wanted to throw the book at him for every wrongdoing and hurt he had inflicted on others. "I'll do my best, but I can't make any promises. That's up to the judge and jury."

Phillip let out a deep breath. "John Roberts paid a healthy sum of money to the kidnappers for them to kidnap his own daughter, and they paid me to push the paperwork through."

The confirmation of his suspicions hit Ben like a physical blow, despite the lack of surprise. "But why? Why not just divorce his wife and share custody?"

"The woman he wanted to marry, Tiffany, couldn't have children. This was their answer. John Roberts figured his wife could still have more children, and he wanted a chance at happiness with his new wife and his daughter."

Everything fell into place. Mandy would be devastated by this news that her own husband had orchestrated the whole thing. Such a travesty of love. One that might set her back another decade, shying away from relationships and love. But who could blame her? "Did John Roberts come back early from his trip and sneak in without Mandy knowing and drug her that night?"

"Yes," Phillip admitted, the single word heavy with guilt.

"Just so you know, Mandy Roberts is the same as Sergeant Mandy Peters of the Crossroads Creek PD."

Phillip sucked in a deep breath. "I'm so sorry. Tell her I'm sorry. She's a good police officer. I can't believe I helped to destroy her life. It was easier not knowing the people," he added, his anguish genuine.

"I'll tell her, and maybe you can tell her yourself one day. Not that an apology can wipe away the pain you've caused everyone." Perhaps there was a chance for Mandy to heal in all this. Forgiveness. It was mostly for the person doing the forgiving so they could move on with their lives and not be consumed by the past. Was this the way for Mandy and her daughter to grow and heal? "What can you tell me about the Bellingham's daughter who was kidnapped six years ago?"

Phillip shook his head. "Not much. They were pretty hush hush about it. Paid extra. I know the child was moved to some place in California with the people who were adopting her. I know they had falsified paperwork to make the girl disappear under one name and reappear under a new name in a new state."

"I can get somebody on that and see if we can track down new adoptions around that time frame. It's a long shot, but worth the manpower to see if we can find the girl and reunite her with her parents. And what of the Hunter kidnapping in Wylie?"

"Once they find out I've told you as much as I have, my life is all but finished anyway. I guess it can't hurt to tell you the rest. It's actually very similar to the Robert's case. It's like I've come full circle. I'm finished." Phillip was withdrawn and Ben was worried he would stop talking and there were still answers he needed.

"What do you mean?" he pressed.

"The girl's father, Bill Hunter, is planning on divorcing his wife. He doesn't want to share custody. I wouldn't be surprised if he's already started divorce proceedings. Seemed he was eager to make it happen and didn't like the idea of waiting to throw off any suspicions of his involvement. Just like John Roberts."

Ben got excited at the possibility of recovering the child. "What can you give us to help find the girl and make sure that her father is brought to justice for this?"

"The child is staying with Hunter's mistress in a country house just outside of Dallas. I heard them talking when they didn't know I could hear. I think it was something like Pineville or Ponvel."

"That will help narrow it down. Thanks. Anything more specific, and how can we prove it's the husband?" Ben would track down this lead and find the child.

"Get a search warrant and check his car. Guy was probably smart enough to ditch the heavy sedative he used on his wife, but you never know. And most likely there will be a large withdrawal from one of his financial institutions that corresponds to when his daughter was kidnapped. Check his flight time home from the business trip to show he was in town. Maybe find out if his mistress was with him or if there even was a business trip. I mean it's all the basics you would already know to check and I don't have anything else to give you."

"What can you tell me about the people you've been working with? Names, numbers, every detail. I need you to write it down. I'm guessing the other cases had other law officers on the inside doing the dirty paperwork to cover the kidnapper's trail. If you know any names, list them on the paper also. And write down everything you've told me so far," he added, shoving a notepad in Phillip's direction. "I've got to make a phone call and I'll be right back. One last thing. I'll need your badge."

Phillip nodded and unclipped his badge, sliding it across the table.

The shell of a man sat before him, but in time, perhaps he would grow from his terrible lapse in judgement and mistakes he'd made. So many people's lives were destroyed but hopefully, some of them could begin healing finally. Thank you, God, for Phillip's cooperation.

Ben stepped out of the interrogation room and posted a guard at the door. He needed someone to track down Bill Hunter's mistress's name and current address, hopefully in Pilverton, a small town outside of Dallas. And it was time to call the social services worker at the children's home and explain what he knew and to coordinate a meeting as soon as possible.

It was time Mandy and her daughter were reunited, and they'd waited long enough.

Chapter Seventeen

BEN DROVE TO MANDY'S place, not entirely sure how the visit would go. He had amazing news for her, but with the positive, there was a huge negative. He parked in the driveway and made his way to the front door, making sure the gate latched behind him in case Frieda got out.

He knocked at her door.

Mandy and Frieda came around from the side of the house, startling him. "Why do you keep showing up at my place?"

"I told you I'd let you know what was going on within forty-eight hours. I'm early by a day." Ben smiled, hoping to ease the tension between them.

"So let's hear it. What's the big investigation and all the secrecy for?" Mandy asked, hands on hips as Frieda ran circles around her feet, looking for attention.

"You might want to sit down," Ben said. How did one break the news? No matter how good it might be, there would be an emotional upheaval.

"I'm fine right where I am. Quit stalling," she snapped.

"The truth is, I was here to investigate the Wylie kidnapping case. It was linked together with seven other kidnappings over the past six years, though it has turned into nine cases in eight years. I was here to investigate the local police departments closest to the last kidnapping."

Mandy frowned. She raised her hand, pushing the hair away from her face and stared at him. "The police departments? I don't understand."

"There was suspicion someone was working on the inside, making it more difficult for the police to track down and put an end to this potential kidnapping ring. It was my job to come here and figure out if there was any truth to the matter," Ben added.

"Let me guess, you found out we're all good officers, right?" Mandy asked.

Ben shook his head. "Sadly, no. In fact, Officer Phillip Williams is under arrest as an accessory in the kidnapping of the Hunter's daughter. He's also an accessory to the kidnapping of the Bellingham's daughter in Austin six years ago. And..."

The color drained from Mandy's face, her eyes widening as tears gathered. "And what?" she prompted, stepping closer.

His heart ached for the pain he was about to cause, even with the joy that would follow. There was no other way to tell her than straight up. "And he is also being charged as an accessory in the kidnapping of Sylvia Roberts. Your daughter," he added, just to make sure she understood the full impact of what he was saying.

"How dare you do this to me?" her anguished cry ripping him to shreds. "Sylvia? Is this some kind of joke? My daughter is Olivia, so it's not my daughter you've found, and I can't believe you would hurt me this way. Making me believe..." She covered her face and turned away.

The misery in her voice cut him to the core. "I would never hurt you, and I made sure of my facts before coming to you with this. Trust me, Sylvia Roberts is the daughter Tiffany and John Roberts raised, but she's also your daughter."

Mandy spun back around, her mouth gaping open.

"Phillip Williams has confessed to sabotaging the police reports and investigation in the kidnapping of your daughter, and he's admitted that John came back earlier than you expected and he drugged you, which is why you were so tired and incapable of moving. He's also helping us to locate the children on the cases he assisted," Ben continued, trying to explain while she was intent on listening.

"I can't believe this. You're saying John did this to me?" Her voice trembled in disbelief. Mandy wrapped her arms around her midsection and rocked back and forth, trying to understand the magnitude of his news. "And Olivia..." she squeaked out, her voicing trailing to a hopeful whisper as she clasped her hands together like she was praying.

Ben nodded, more than happy to give her the magnificent news part of this visit. "Yes, Sylvia. We have found her, and she's fine," he said, quick to reassure Mandy.

"Oh my gosh," the words came out as a breathless whisper, as she dropped to her knees. "I can't believe it. All my prayers for all these years..." Her voice broke. "You're telling me they've been answered?" Tears streamed down Mandy's face. Huge sobs racking her body. After several minutes, she pulled herself together enough to look up at him. "Where is she? When can I see her? What happened? You said she was okay. Is that true?"

"Slow down. I've got lots to tell you. Sylvia is in a children's home just outside of Austin, where she was placed with child services a few months ago."

Mandy frowned, her head tilted to one side, deep in thought. Confusion clouded her expression. "I don't understand. Why is she in a children's home? Didn't they want her anymore?" Mandy stood and moved to the porch and sat down, as if it was all too much to take in.

Ben followed. "John and Tiffany Roberts died in a car accident a few months ago. Their daughter Sylvia had no relatives come forward, and they placed her in a children's home to allow time to locate any relative or eventually place her in foster care."

"Why do you keep calling her Sylvia? My daughter's name is Olivia."

"That's what I'm trying to explain. You see, John hired someone to kidnap your daughter and then he blamed it on you to make it look good when he left. He was having an affair with Tiffany Roberts and Tiffany couldn't have children of her own, so he devised a plan to take his own daughter. Apparently, he figured you could still have children and that justified it. I'm so sorry." Ben could tell it was all finally coming together in her brain and she was having a hard time swallowing the bitter pill that came with the amazing news.

"I can't believe this. I know John and I didn't get along but the fact that he would do something so hateful? I just can't believe it. And I can't believe he got away with it. Wait, you said he died, so that's truly my Olivia at the children's home. How did you figure this out? How do you know all your information is right?"

"It was a matter of doing some investigating, tying together some loose ends that weren't making sense. It started after you told me about your daughter's kidnapping in Austin.

Your case wasn't linked with the other cases because it included an infant daughter, and all the others were over the age of three, not to mention, it was two years prior to all the other cases. But it got me digging deeper, which is why I was checking into your background. I had to know everything about the kidnapping, but I didn't want to upset you. I didn't want to give you false hope or promises for something that might not be what you would want, in case it wasn't your daughter. But a friend of mine in Austin PD sent me some records on John and Tiffany and the accident.

Apparently John, right before he died, kept saying Sylvia. Find Deedee. Sylvia. Find Deedee. That's why everybody was looking for a relative or a family friend or someone named Deedee, and it wasn't until you told me it was your nickname that I put it all together and knew for sure. I just had to make one hundred percent sure—for your sake. It would seem John was trying to do the right thing by returning your daughter to you. And then, of course, there's the fact I've seen her picture, and she's the spitting image of you."

Mandy stood up again and started pacing. "She is?" Joy lighting her eyes with the question.

"Yes. Beautiful sapphire blue eyes, long, curly brown hair with honey gold highlights, and a dainty nose.

The excitement of knowing her daughter had been found was like a glow on Mandy's face as she lifted her head and said a silent prayer. There was much to be thankful for.

"When can I meet her? What do I need to do to bring her home?"

"I tried to arrange a meeting for this evening after I talked with you, but based on the input from the social worker, it will not happen the way I planned." Ben was torn about the decision. He understood both sides of the equation, but in the end, he had to trust the professionals knew what they were doing. He'd never been a parent.

"What do you mean? Can I go see my daughter? I need to go get her. She has no business in a children's home when I'm here. I'm her mother," Mandy said, her smile vanished just as quickly as it had come.

"Yes, I understand. But the social worker is concerned about your daughter's emotional upheaval when she learns the truth. The game plan is to get the two of you together tomorrow, but the social worker wants to speak with you first. They want this to be a smooth process and done in a way that is in the best interest of Sylvia."

Mandy frowned. "Of course, being with me would be the best thing for Olivia."

"Sylvia," he corrected gently. "That was one thing the case worker was clear on. You can't go in and just change her name. There will come a time when you can tell her the truth about the past, but it's not now. She's only eight years old."

"I know how old she is. What do they propose we do, because I'm not walking away from my daughter."

Liam knew Mandy wouldn't like the plan, but it was better coming from him than her finding out through the cold efficiency of the social worker. "The caseworker is hoping that you will agree to adopt her. They've agreed to let her live with you until the paperwork is finalized based on character witness assessments provided by both me and Chief Jackson. Sort of like foster care. It's all about the best interest of the child and her emotional well-being, and they agree it would be good to keep the two of you together and allow the bonding to begin. This is an unusual situation and since you've not been a part of the child's life, through no fault of your own, they want the judge to award you legal custody as part of the process to make this final."

"*Argghh*. This is crazy! She's my daughter. I haven't seen her in eight years. She was ripped from my home in the middle of the night, and now you want me to adopt my own daughter?" Mandy was pacing the yard furiously, clearly on the verge of an emotional breakdown.

Ben moved closer and stopped her. He moved to pull her in his arms, wanting to comfort her.

Mandy pulled back. "No." She drew up taller, more resolute. "Have the woman contact me and I'll do whatever they want me to do for my daughter's sake. But that's where this ends. You. Me. All this time, and you couldn't tell me you thought you had found my daughter. You kept all this from me. John was full of lies and cheating. I just want nothing to do with living a life of lies, and everything between you and I has been based on lies. I need to trust whoever I share my life with, and you've proven you don't trust me above your job. It's time for you to go. Just let them know how to contact me. I need to focus on my daughter now, nothing else. Thank you for what you've done, and I'm sorry things can't be different between us, but I can't undo the past."

Ben's heart plummeted, her words so final. And true. He had lied to her, but for a good cause. "I did what I did to protect you. If I was wrong, I'm sorry. I only did what I thought was best—for you." Ben turned and walked across the lawn and through the gate, the latch clicking with a finality that echoed in his heart.

As he drove away, he realized some victories came at a high a price. He'd found Mandy's daughter, but lost her trust—and perhaps her heart. Yet somehow, he knew this part of God's plan, even if he couldn't see the entire picture yet.

His time in Crossroads Creek was over.

Chapter

Eighteen

♥

T HE HIGHWAY STRETCHED ENDLESSLY before Mandy as she drove toward Austin, her heart racing with nervous anticipation unlike anything she had ever experienced. After a sleepless night, thinking about all that had happened and why, she still couldn't believe she would meet her daughter today. It seemed so surreal.

She followed the GPS directions and turned into the driveway at her destination. The large, two-story colonial home featured both a columned front porch stoop over the doorway, and an add-on massive side porch that would appeal to children. Great for rainy day activities outside. The well-maintained grounds and freshly painted trim offered a reassuring first impression. At least Sylvia had a nice roof over her head the past few months. Mandy hoped the caregivers were nice as well. Her heart ached at the thought of her daughter facing John and Tiffany's deaths alone, her entire world upended with no family support. She would do everything in her power to rectify what her daughter had been through.

Mandy walked in the front door and approached the receptionist's desk, the wood floors creaking. The woman's gray hair and kind eyes put her more at ease. "Hi, I'm Mandy Peters and I'm here to meet with Laura Haskins."

"Good morning, Miss Peters, we've been expecting you." Several young kids raced through the area and up the staircase. "Slow down, Ginny and Krista! You know the rules for inside behavior."

The children halted in their tracks. "Yes, Mrs. Drummond," they answered in unison before continuing up the stairs at a slow pace. Almost an exaggerated slow pace, as though they were having fun at the older woman's expense. Kids will be kids.

"Sorry about that. I'll show you to Mrs. Haskins' office." The woman grabbed a cane propped up next to her desk and started down the hall. "Here you go," she said, leaning inside the doorway. "Miss Peters is here to see you."

"Good. Come in, come in." Laura Haskins rose from behind her desk, her silver-streaked hair framing her face. Her pleasant smile was welcoming as she crossed the room.

"Thanks for seeing me on such short notice, but I'm sure you understand my urgency," Mandy said, taking the seat in front of the woman's oversized desk Laura indicated for her to use.

"Yes, of course, dear. Such a tragedy for everyone concerned. Most of all Sylvia."

Mandy's hands twisted in her lap. "Can you tell me what you know about everything? There's still a lot I don't know or understand."

"Of course, dear. It's a lot to take in, but Texas Ranger Calhoun has certainly covered all his bases. He explained everything to me. A sad story, but it seems to have a happy ending."

"Did you just say Texas Ranger Calhoun? As in Ben Calhoun?"

"Why, yes. That's his name. What a nice man. You didn't know?"

"No. I mean, at first I didn't know he was undercover, but then I found out and he told me his name, but I had no idea he was a Texas Ranger. I figured he was a Dallas detective or working for the Texas DPS." She couldn't believe this new twist in all that happened, and of course, she never gave him the chance to tell her.

Laura went over the entire story, or the parts and pieces she knew. Mostly, she talked about Sylvia since her arrival at the home and how she was doing. The revelation that John altered their daughter's birth certificate and parentage was another devastating blow she hadn't expected. Apparently, if you paid the right people, it was easy to go from July 5th to July 15th and doctor up the document to change the mother's name.

Understanding why John would do this to her was still the part she couldn't wrap her head around. She couldn't fathom that he would inflict so much pain and stoop to such low limits for what he considered happiness.

"Thank you for sharing all that with me," she said, when it seemed Laura had finished. "It's good to know Sylvia's done well since her arrival."

"She's been through a lot but is a super smart young lady. I hope you understand why I'm worried, and that you'll agree with my decisions regarding Sylvia's immediate future and how we proceed with reuniting the two of you," Laura said, pouring a cup of water and offering it to Mandy.

"Thanks. I have thought it over, and of course, I will do anything you ask. All I want is what's best for my daughter and to hold her in my arms again." She took a sip of the cool water to wet her parched throat. Now that the moment was finally here, she was even more nervous. What if Sylvia didn't like her?

It was something she hadn't considered. What if her daughter didn't want a new mother? The very idea ached deep in her heart.

"Good. I've prepared Sylvia for the meeting. She knows you are visiting today to meet her, and that you would like to adopt her. I've explained that her input is valuable to us and that we want to make sure she's totally comfortable with everything happening. Normally, things don't move along this quickly, but considering the situation, I'm trying to make it work. You have excellent character references coming from some high authority officials that will help expedite this process."

"I appreciate all that you're doing for me. For us. My daughter and I."

"Yes, well then, let's go meet her. She's out back playing in the yard. I'll put you in the family room to wait for us. It's a room where children and adults can meet without curious eyes and distractions all around them.

"Oh...Okay," Mandy said, her breath coming faster as her heart raced.

"Are you okay?" Laura asked, as Mandy slowed her pace going down the hall.

"Truthfully, I'm nervous and excited all at the same time. I want to scoop her up in my arms and hug her for weeks, but I understand it would only scare her."

"I trust you'll do fine. Relax and have a seat and I'll be right back with Sylvia."

Mandy couldn't stop fidgeting as she rubbed her hands together, trying to displace some of the nervous energy. The door opened and her daughter walked in. There was no way to stop the tears that filled her eyes, whether or not Mrs. Easkins liked it. This was simply nothing she could control or stop.

Liam was right...Sylvia looked exactly like her.

Her daughter stared back at Mandy, wide eyed, and one hand twisting her ponytail.

"Sylvia, this is Mandy Peters, the woman I told you about last night."

"It's nice to meet you, Sylvia," Mandy said, unable to believe this was really happening.

Sylvia tilted her head, studying Mandy's face. "Your eyes look like mine. And your face and hair too. How come?"

Laura's eyes bore into her, holding Mandy in check from blurting out the truth. "It is surprising how much we look like each other, but as to being related..." Mandy shrugged, unwilling to lie.

"But why do you want me?" Sylvia asked, scuffing her sneakers on the carpet. "I don't even know you." She glanced up at Mrs. Haskins. "Right?"

"I knew your father, and he wanted you with me after your parents died in the car accident."

Sylvia's forehead wrinkled in confusion. She turned to Mrs. Haskins, moving closer to the woman. "My dad never told me about anyone named Mandy. Never ever."

"She's telling the truth, dear," Laura reassured Sylvia.

Mandy needed to find a way to connect with her daughter. "Your father and I had a falling out and didn't see each other for a long time. He used to call me Deedee." She leaned forward as if to share a secret. "And guess what? They only just figured out your father meant me when he kept telling people to find me for you."

Sylvia took a few steps forward, curiosity overtaking her shyness. "Deedee?" She giggled. "That's a funny name. So, you knew about me? Right?"

"I did. I also know your dad loved you to the moon and back," Mandy said, smiling at her beautiful daughter, willing her to understand how much she cared.

Sylvia's entire face lit up. "That's what he said to me every night. Even when I was too big for bedtime stories!" She spun around, as though she were a ballerina.

The memory brought both joy and tears, Mandy quickly wiping them away. "Do you remember any other special things you did with your dad?"

It was as though a veil had been lifted, and joy filled the little girl's heart. Sylvia moved closer and the two of them sat down. "We did everything together. I remember when he made me mickey mouse pancakes for breakfast. And we went to the park and he'd push me on the swing. So where do you live?"

Mandy's heart did a somersault when her daughter smiled. She had to trust in God that everything would work out. Why else would He bring them back together again? "In Crossroads Creek, Texas."

"Is that far away? Do they have horses? I've always wanted a horse. Do you have a horse?" Sylvia was warming up now, the questions tumbling out. "What's your house like? Do you have any pets? I've always wanted one, but my mom always said no."

"Crossroads Creek is a small town in Tumbleweed County. I'm a police officer there." Or at least she was until two days ago.

Sylvia's eyes grew wide as saucers, intently listening.

"And yes, there are lots of horses, though I don't have one myself. But I have a puppy named Frieda. She loves to play and you two will get along great."

"A puppy?" Sylvia's eyes lit up, then bit her lip, suddenly serious again. "Are you sure you want me to live with you? Cause I'd really like a puppy and that would be so cool."

Mandy's heart ached at the question. "Absolutely sure. And we can even look into getting some horseback riding lessons together. I would love to learn to ride."

"Goody. Did you hear that Mrs. Haskins?" Sylvia asked, her smile warming Mandy's heart.

"I did. That would be lovely, dear." Mrs. Haskins stepped in closer. "Perhaps you two would like to go to lunch and get to know one another better, and then we can finalize the arrangements. We don't normally rush things, but considering it was your father's wishes that you be in Miss Peters' care, we are making exceptions to the rules. Ms. Peter's is quite an amazing woman from what I hear and you two should get along famously."

Laura's praise came as a surprise, but it was nice knowing she was firmly in her court. "Lunch sounds wonderful. Are you interested, Sylvia?" Mandy asked, more than ready to be alone with her daughter without Laura's over-sight. She couldn't hold her baby anymore, but she could talk to her and soon enough, hug her soon to be nine-year-old daughter. The best years of Sylvia's life were ahead of her, and Mandy wanted to enjoy every one of them.

Sylvia nodded. "Cool. I'm hungry."

Last night, Mandy realized that as much as she wanted to hate John for what he did, she couldn't. After praying about it, it occurred to her that at least Sylvia had her father the whole time she'd been missing And based on Sylvia's comments about her dad, it would seem John had been a loving father. What he did was wrong, but now Mandy was the one who would spend time with their daughter. And for that, she was grateful.

After Laura delivered her safety speech, set a return time, and made sure Sylvia was buckled correctly in the back seat, Mandy started the car and drove away.

She glanced up occasionally into the rearview mirror, still unable to believe her daughter was back in her life. Sylvia had brightened considerably and was quite a talkative girl with lots of questions. One by one, Mandy answered them all, asking a few questions of her own. They headed for Toni's, an Italian restaurant nearby, having discovered their mutual affinity for pizza and pasta.

This was tied for the best day ever in her life—the other being the day her daughter was born.

At the restaurant, Sylvia couldn't seem to sit still. She had so many questions about everything, not just Mandy's life. Questions about the ceiling fan. The pictures on the wall. What other people were eating for lunch.

Mandy did a quick check of her email as they waited for their pizza and drinks. She was surprised to see one from the Appleton Police Department, one of the places where she put in an application. She scanned the letter, and with a satisfied smile, leaned back in the booth.

"What's going on? You have a really big smile on your face," Sylvia said.

Mandy grinned. "I am. I've met you. We're having lunch. And if you say yes, I'll have a new daughter. And on top of all that, I got a job offer at another police department. Life is good."

"Are you going to take it? Does that mean you'll be moving? Crossroads Creek sounded awesome the way you described it on the way here."

The server dropped off their iced teas. "Thanks." She turned back to Sylvia. "I don't know about the job. Probably not. I've got you to consider now, and I'd rather spend some time with you and do some fun things."

Sylvia's eyes widened. "You must be super rich," she exclaimed, then quickly covered her mouth. "Sorry, daddy says it s not polite to talk about money."

"It's okay. The answer is no, I'm not super rich, but I have worked a lot over the last eight years and didn't take vacations or do much else. I've got a lot of money saved up. Plenty enough to tide us over for a while. Besides, I was thinking I should get out of law enforcement and perhaps switch to being a paralegal. Safer job with you to consider and regular hours." Not to mention that she didn't get the promotion she wanted, and it would take years for another chance like that to come along. Though she wondered what would happen now when Ben Calhoun returned to Dallas.

Sylvia shrugged. "Okay."

"You've mentioned your dad a few times, but you say little about your mother. Were you two close?" Mandy couldn't help but ask, though she was unsure how she wanted Sylvia to answer.

"Mom was okay. She didn't like doing kid stuff much. Like when I wanted to build a blanket fort or play dress-up princess, she always said she had a headache. But daddy always played with me. He even let me do a pretty-pretty princess makeover on him." Sylvia's responses seemed overloaded with a complexity of emotions.

It broke Mandy's heart to hear that Tiffany might have been jealous of Sylvia and couldn't reconcile that she wasn't her real mother. Or at least, that's what it sounded like to Mandy.

"So, we agree, I'll turn down the job and we can do some of the fun things you've always wanted to do before you start school in the fall. What are some of your favorite things?" Mandy asked.

Sylvia's face lit up as she counted off on her fingers. "I love swimming and riding bikes. And drawing pictures. I'm really good at drawing horses and now you're going to let me learn how to ride. I'm so excited. Oh, and I love to play games, but I hate losing. My favorite is Monopoly with the electronic machine thingy that goes in the middle. *Hmmm*, let's see," she said, tapping her cheek. "I love pizza, but you already know that. And I love ice cream, but the green stuff with minty chocolate chips is my favorite. My favorite color is purple, and I can do a cartwheel. Want me to show you?"

"Maybe later." Mandy laughed, her heart full of love with her daughter's animated chatter.

The pepperoni, mushroom, and olive pizza was delivered moments later, ending any other immediate discussions as they concentrated on eating. Sylvia, it seemed, even liked the same pizza as Mandy. After eight long years of prayers and heartache, God had brought her daughter back into her life. The journey ahead might not always be easy, but they would face it together.

Chapter Nineteen

♥

BEN FINISHED THE DEBRIEFING reports and hit save. He closed his laptop and looked around the office, knowing the undercover part of his investigation was over. Mandy's empty desk brought him no joy as he recalled their shared laughs and morning coffee, or the way her eyes lit up when they discussed a case.

As he gathered his things, Ben said a silent prayer of gratitude. This assignment had brought him more than just another closed case—it brought him back to his roots, back to his faith, and somehow, back to life.

He would continue to follow up on what they knew about the kidnappers to round them up and put them all behind bars. At least their operation would have trouble staying under the radar now, and it was his hope it would be an end to the group permanently, and that children were safer.

There was an entire team now assigned to investigating all the other officers on the police reports of the kidnapping cases. If any officer wasn't cooperative and wanting to help them rule them out as a suspect, the judge was all too happy to issue a search warrant based on probable cause. They also had a team leading the search for the missing children and already closing in on the most recent case. Hopefully, by nightfall the Hunter child would be back with her mother, and Bill Hunter behind bars.

Ben made his way to Chief Jackson's office and entered. Knowing this was goodbye to a place that had unexpectedly become home again left him cold. He entered without knocking, seeing as the door was wide open.

"Nice work, Ranger Calhoun," the chief said, all too aware that the need for caution and an alias were gone.

"Thanks. Mandy's case was really the saving grace on this investigation. I just wanted to say goodbye, as I'm headed back to close up the house and then on to Dallas."

The chief came around the desk, closing the distance between them. A move he rarely made. "You know, there's a place for you here on the CCPD if you want it. We could make that captain's promotion official."

The offer came as a surprise. A compliment for sure coming from Chief Jackson, but his happy moment lasted all of two seconds. "I appreciate your confidence in me, but you need to get Mandy back in here for the job. She worked hard for the promotion and deserves it." In fact, the job would be hers already if it hadn't been for his interference.

The chief nodded. "Very true, but Officer Peters quit. I heard she's got applications in other areas, and I've been getting reference calls. It would seem the Applewood PD has already made her an offer. Disappointing to lose both of you, but in the end, for a good cause."

"Sir, just talk to her and try. You know this is where her heart is. Please," Ben added, wanting to put everything back to right for Mandy.

"Absolutely. Again, thanks for all you did. The state of Texas will be much safer with this group of thugs off the streets and behind bars."

Ben nodded, the two men shaking hands. It was a firm, meaningful gesture between equals. "My life will be forever changed by this assignment." With those words hanging in the air, he turned and left.

He dialed Terrance's number knowing what he needed to do.

"Hey there. I've been meaning to call you and let you know I was back in town. Figured we could go get something to eat while you're in town," Terrance said.

"That would be great, but our timing is lousy. I'm headed back to Dallas shortly. Which is why I am calling."

"What do you mean?" Terrance asked.

"I want you to sell the ranch. It makes no sense to hang onto something when I don't plan to be back. " The words brought him no comfort.

"Are you sure? Twenty years later and then suddenly you want to sell? Doesn't make any sense."

"It does to me. It's about closure." Ben let out a heavy breath of air.

"All right then. I'll email you some documents to sign and get a property appraisal for you to review so that we can set a price. I'm sure it will sell quickly as property doesn't change hands around here very often."

"Thanks."

"Take care, Ben," Terrance said.

"You do the same." Ben hung up the phone.

There was nothing left for Ben here, though he enjoyed being back in Crossroads Creek, and even more so, being home again. The old homestead offered him whispers of his childhood, like the creak of the porch swing where his mother used to read him stories and gaze out at the stars on a moonlit night. The immense oak tree where his father built a double-decker treehouse that Ben hid away in when he got in trouble. And then there were the initials he carved on the fireplace mantel, much to his parents 'dismay. It was his way of marking his place in a world that most of the time he didn't feel as though he fit into.

He'd stayed away thinking it was for the best, but now he understood how wrong he had been. There was an unexpected peace here that made him loath to sell, but he couldn't justify keeping it either.

Mandy was a big part of the difference in him, though most of the credit went to God. Opening his heart, God had shown him the way to heal, forgive, and love again. Unfortunately, the woman he loved wanted nothing to do with him.

If only he could change the stars.

Mandy watched as Sylvia slept, the soft glow of the nightlight casting gentle shadows across her daughter's face. A strand of honey-brown hair fell across Sylvia's cheek, and it was hard not to brush it away after all the years she had been denied the luxury. At some point, she might get more comfortable and not be a helicopter mom, but if there was ever a reason, she had it. No questions asked.

It was times like now, after her daughter had gone to bed at night, that she missed Liam and his laughter. The way his eyes crinkled at the corners when he smiled. The way he always seemed to know what she needed. The moments when she thought about his kisses and his kindness. Or the way he smiled when he delivered her a cup of coffee at the office.

Most of all, she thought about how he found her daughter and that she owed him a huge debt of gratitude. But it didn't stop at gratitude. Mandy cared deeply for Liam, or rather Ben. It was hard making the switch, but she was trying. The name might be different, but the man who had slowly worked his way past her defenses was real.

Her cell phone rang, interrupting her thoughts. Chief Jackson's name flashed across the screen. It took her off guard and she was instantly worried. "Hello," she said, holding her breath.

"Good evening, Officer Peters." The tone of his voice put her at ease. This wasn't a bad call with bad news.

"Just Mandy, sir. Please." He wasn't her boss anymore and she would like to think of Bill Jackson as a friend.

"Mandy it is. Thanks. Am I disrupting anything?" he asked.

"No. My daughter is in bed, and I was just going to relax for a bit and unwind. What's up?"

"I'm pleased everything is working out with you and Sylvia. Such a blessing. The reason for my call is that I want to formally offer you the captain's job. I tried to tell you to give me a few weeks, and I'd figure out something, because I knew the new captain wasn't sticking around. It was always meant to be your job, as I was recently reminded. Even though you quit, I want you to know the door is wide open for your return."

Shock coursed through her veins, her heart pounding in her chest. This was the promotion she'd worked hard for, putting in days and nights, her dedication to the team unparalleled. Elation surged through her veins, a sense of satisfaction settling over her. "I'm honored, sir. Truly I am. Who did the reminding?" she couldn t help but ask, pretty certain she knew the answer.

"Ranger Calhoun. He left this afternoon to head back to Dallas, and I would love it if you came back to work for me. Please say yes, Mandy. You've earned this promotion."

Mandy wanted to do a happy dance, but two things held her in check. First, knowing Ben had already left was a void in her heart she couldn't help but feel. She knew she had used her anger as an excuse to run from those feelings. She didn't want to give up control over her life to anyone, and she definitely didn't want to be around someone she didn't trust. Except Ben had been doing his job and helping her. Instead of hugging and thanking him for the wonderful gift he'd given her, she'd tossed him to the curb, a move she now regretted.

Second, she had already turned down the Appleton PD and would now need to do the same for Crossroads Creek. Another love had stolen her heart. *Sylvia.* Every decision Mandy made would be centered on what was best for her daughter. And right now, that was spending time with her to forge the bond that would connect them at a deeper level.

"Are you still there, Mandy?" the chief asked when she didn't respond.

They were tough words to say but she would say them. "I'm here. And I'm sorry, but I need to kindly say no to your offer."

"But I thought—"

"I wanted the promotion. Past tense. Now, everything in my life has changed. Having my daughter back and spending time with her is my top priority and, in fact, I don't plan to go back to work anywhere for at least six months. Even then, I'm not sure what I want to do. Maybe I'll enroll in a paralegal course or something like that. I need to be available for all the moments in Sylvia's life that I missed. Her first day of school, parent-teacher conferences, soccer games. Everything."

"I see. You're an outstanding police officer and the CCPD will miss you. If you ever change your mind, you're always welcome to come back to the department. I'll have to hire someone for the captain's job, mind you, but would love to have you back on the force."

Kind words that comforted her. She was making big changes, and it was nice to know there was a backup plan in place. "Thank you, sir. I appreciate the offer and will keep it in mind. Right now, I don't know my next step, but I won't make any decisions until Sylvia starts school in the fall."

"I understand."

"Oh, and sir, if you want my recommendation for who you promote, I'm willing to go over the scope of the other officers in the department," Mandy offered.

"Enough with the sir. Call me Bill. All my friends do. As to your suggestion, I'll have to pass on your kind offer, seeing as I've already got someone in mind. Take care, Mandy, and I wish you the best."

She wondered who the lucky officer was that would get her promotion. Hopefully, they did an amazing job and deserved the trust Chief Jackson was putting in them. After they hung up, a sense of peace washed over Mandy. She had been blessed in so many ways.

Returning to Sylvia's bedside, Mandy kneeled beside her sleeping daughter. "Thank you, God," she whispered, tears of gratitude sliding down her cheeks. "Thank you for bringing her back to me, for keeping her safe, for giving me strength through all these years. And thank you for sending Ben, even if I was too scared to see the blessing he could be." She reached out, finally giving in to the urge to smooth that errant strand of hair from Sylvia's face. Her daughter stirred slightly but didn't wake, and Mandy's heart swelled with love.

Chapter Twenty

TENTATIVELY ACCEPT. TWO WORDS that held a wealth of meaning for Ben. They were the words he gave Chief Jackson in response to his offer for the position of captain. His second offer. The phrase carried both hope and hesitation.

Ben still couldn't believe Mandy had turned down the job. Though when the chief explained why, it made perfect sense. Her daughter was in her life now and she would be an amazing mother. He respected her all the more, as the decision couldn't have been an easy one. It spoke volumes about her character, her faith, and her commitment to make up for lost time with Sylvia.

With Veronica back in Dallas and her stalker behind bars courtesy of the fingerprints they lifted off the letter, Ben had nothing holding him in Dallas. He would always be available for Veronica if she needed him, but she had been most encouraging when he explained about the job offer and why he was torn about accepting the position. It was Veronica who made him see reason. If he loved Mandy, it was a rare gift, and one he should be willing to fight for. She also didn't pull any punches about a Texas Ranger being afraid of telling a woman he loved her.

The thought of moving back to the ranch permanently checked all his boxes. Stability. Less danger. Peace. Family. Belonging. *Home.* The only thing missing was having Mandy in the picture to make his homecoming complete.

He loved her enough that although he wanted to say yes, he wouldn't. Not yet, anyway. Ben wouldn't do anything to upset her, knowing she had been through enough and he wouldn't disrupt her new found peace and joy. More than that, he hoped she would find it in her heart to give him another chance. For them as a team. Not just any team...a couple. They didn't work together anymore and there was nothing holding them back. *Except their hearts.*

The Welcome to Crossroads Creek stirred him to life, unable to deny that he couldn't wait to see Mandy. Ben hoped she would find it in her heart to forgive him and give him five minutes to talk. Long enough to apologize. He drove straight to her place, anxious to see her.

Frieda barked, running up and down the fence line. He latched the gate, and in no time, Frieda was at his feet, barking up at him. He bent down to pet the pup, getting licked in the process. "You must be on a pee break," he said, rubbing behind her ears. He stood, brushed off his jeans, and moved to the porch, raising his hand to knock.

The door opened, and he stood face to face with Sylvia Roberts. It was incredible how much she looked like her mother. Her freckled face and wide grin gave him hope that her mother might be equally receptive to his visit. "Hi! You're playing with my puppy!" Sylvia said, bouncing up and down like she was playing hopscotch, ponytail swinging. "Frieda likes you. Are you a friend of Mandy's? She's my new mom, you know."

"Yes, I'm a friend of your mothers. My name is Ben Calhoun, and I was hoping—"

"Sylvia, who's at the door?" Mandy asked, her heels clicking on the hall floor as she approached.

"There's a cowboy guy out here playing with Frieda!" Sylvia said, turning back to Ben. "I can tell because of your cowboy hat." She grinned.

"I know we haven't discussed this yet, but please don't answer the door again by—" Mandy pushed the door open wide, and fell silent, clearly surprised to see him.

"Good afternoon, Mandy," Ben said, shooting her a smile to ease the tension.

"Yes, Sylvia, he's a friend. Ben, this is my daughter, Sylvia." Mandy said, stepping out onto the porch, Sylvia right behind her.

"Nice to meet you, young lady."

"Are you really a cowboy?" Sylvia asked.

"I was when I was younger, and then I moved to the city. But the hat still fits, and I love the country life, and love to ride horses, so I'm guessing that's a yes. Though mucking stalls still isn't my thing." Ben chuckled.

"Cool. But what's mucking mean? It sounds disgusting," Sylvia asked.

"It is. It's cleaning up horse poop."

Mandy laughed. "The trick is not to step in it. Otherwise, it sticks with you a lot longer," she teased, clearly remembering the run in with the pig manure.

"I want to learn to ride a horse, but I'm with you—no mucking." Sylvia scrunched up her face in distaste.

"Sylvia, honey, why don't you take Frieda into the house and give us a few minutes to chat."

"Sure thing. Come on, Frieda. Let's go." The puppy ran across the yard, eager for attention from Sylvia. The two were quite a pair.

She reminded him of Brianna. His little sister was always full of energy and eager to play. Liam no longer shed a tear or tried to shove aside the memories when he thought of his sister. Instead, he embraced them to celebrate Brianna's life, knowing she was playing in heaven and in a beautiful place filled with love.

"What brings you to Crossroads Creek? Chief Jackson said you had gone back to Dallas."

Ben nodded. "I did. Some things have changed, and I was hoping to talk with you about them."

"I'm glad you're here, Ben. I wanted to talk to you also, but wasn't sure you wouldn't hang up on me after the way I treated you." Her words gave him hope. She didn't hate him for sure.

"You can always talk to me. Your reaction was understandable, and I should have trusted you with the truth. Which is why I'm here. See, I was offered the captain's job you didn't want, yet totally deserve. I have tentatively accepted but will only finalize the decision if my being in town won't upset you. You mean a lot to me, whether or not you understand that, and I truly want what's best for you."

Mandy smiled and reached out to touch his arm. "Maybe we should start over. I'm so sorry I got angry with you. I realize you were simply doing your job, and it wasn't personal. I reacted badly and should have trusted you. The problem is, you scared me because I cared about you, and I knew you could hurt me. I pushed you away to protect my heart."

"So does that mean you've forgiven me for the deceit?" Ben asked.

Mandy shook her head. "There's nothing to forgive. That's what I mean."

"So do you mind if I accept the job and move to Crossroads Creek?" he asked, unable to believe how well this was going. It looked like he was moving home...for good. Adrenaline surged, his heart pounding with anticipation.

"I would love it if you accepted and moved here. And by the way, the black hair suits you. More natural." Mandy's smile touched his heart with warmth.

"Thanks, though I was just getting used to the blond," he teased. "Guess I won't be needing a disguise since I'll be leaving the Rangers."

"What about your ranch house? I saw it was for sale," Mandy said. Ben pulled out his phone and typed out a text to Terrance.

Ben: Take the house off the market please. It's not for sale anymore.

"Not anymore." He grinned.

"I need to tell you something else. I've been so busy and happy with Sylvia, but I also miss having you around." Her gaze never left his face, her eyes echoing her words.

Mandy missed him, and not just as a partner at work. Only a foolish man would waste another minute before telling the woman he loved how much he cared about her. "Well, then, that makes this easy," Ben said.

"What's that?" she asked.

He stepped closer and pulled her into his arms, his hand cupping her cheek softly before kissing her. *He was finally home.*

"Does this mean what I think it means?" she asked, when he finally pulled back and smiled down at her.

"It means I'm tired of hiding that I love you. I want a chance to explore this connection we have together. I feel a sense of peace knowing you're in my life," Ben said, grinning down at her, and loving the light shining in her eyes. "And when I was in Dallas, I was lonely and feeling like a piece of me was missing."

"I want that too," she added shyly. "Though please understand, I have Sylvia to consider in everything."

Ben nodded. "I know, and that's all part of this. She seems like a great kid, and I'd love to get to know her better."

"Absolutely." Mandy nodded, her smile growing wider.

"Since we agree honesty is most important, there's one other thing you should know before we continue our journey together."

"What's that?" Mandy asked

"I'm not against having a family down the road." Ben shot her a wink.

"As in, you want kids? I mean, I don't know what to say," she said, biting her lower lip in the most endearing way that made him want to kiss her again.

"As in, I'm not against us becoming a family in the future. Marriage. You, me, and Sylvia. A family. I think it's better to know expectations before a relationship develops too far, especially given I led you to believe otherwise when we first met."

"Oh, phew, I thought you meant like kids of your own."

"That too. If we decide to get married, I'm open to more kids. What about you?" Ben asked. He never thought he would say the words, but they were true.

Mandy nodded and grinned. "I'm all in, if it's the path God has chosen for us."

Sylvia was a true gem, and Mandy was proud of her daughter. She had been over the moon when Ben bought a few horses to fill his barn, a gentle palomino mare named Sunshine for Sylvia, and two quarter horses. Star was for Mandy, and Storm was for Ben. The offer of lessons was well received and watching Sylvia's confidence grow with each ride filled her and Ben's heart with joy. It was a chance for the three of them to bond, and afterward, time for her and Ben to share moments together as a couple. Late nights on the porch, talking and stargazing as he shared his surprising knowledge of the constellations. the Texas sky stretching endlessly above them.

Best of all, her daughter loved games—something else they had in common. Scrabble. Monopoly. Charades. You name it; they played. Mandy grew up playing board games and she missed the interactions and laughter. Not anymore. Ben, who hadn't played games in twenty years, suddenly found himself back in the saddle again. First with Veronica's children, and now with her and Sylvia. Turns out, his competitive streak was a mile wide and matched Sylvia's.

Crossroads Creek wasn't the most happening place when it came to crime, and Ben was enjoying the slower pace and spending a lot of time at his place fixing it up.

Tonight, however, they were doing something totally different. Ben had invited them to the line dancing event being held at the community center, a tradition that dated back more years than Ben could remember. A local band volunteered every year, and the town all came out to learn new dances, laugh, and simply have a good time with friends and neighbors.

They pulled into a parking spot and made their way to the center. Folks were coming from every direction, ready for the big event. Mandy never attended, as her entire focus had been on work. Sylvia had never done any line dancing and wasn't even sure what it entailed. They were both in for a treat. Ben claimed he wasn't the joining type back when he was younger, though he promised he wouldn't pull a sideliner this evening since it was his idea.

"Good to see you here, Mandy," her friend Jenna said, hugging her.

"Thanks. Ben wouldn't take no for an answer, but then he also had Sylvia on his side." Mandy laughed. She would never have thought she would find overflowing happiness again, but she had been wrong.

"Good for them. It's about time you took part. Officer Peters was against fun before, but now, I'm loving the new Mandy with Sylvia and Ben in her life. Good things come in threes, they say," her friend teased.

"I'm counting my blessings, trust me. Whatever comes my way, I've learned to be grateful."

Jenna hugged her. "Come on let's dance."

"What do we do, Miss Jenna?" Sylvia asked.

"Follow me and just make sure you're surrounded by people who look like they know what they are doing." Jenna laughed. "Then copy them."

"You heard the expert. Let's go," Mandy said, the three of them following Jenna out onto the dance floor.

The trick, it seemed, was to follow the other's lead, and when they turned, you followed the new people in front of you and to the sides. It was certainly an easy way to learn and have fun.

"I love this," Sylvia said, the laughter in her eyes a wonderful sight.

"Me too. Too bad it's only an annual event," Mandy said, enjoying herself in a way she hadn't thought possible. Surrounded by folks from town, people who all knew her name. People who said hello, and cast their worries away for the night.

Ben grinned, dipping the front of his Stetson down a little lower. "Well, ma'am, I'm sure I can find us another place with line dancing for families. Or maybe we can have a good-old-fashioned barn dance when I finish fixing the ranch up," Ben said, shooting her a wink as they waited for the next song.

"I like the sound of the barn dance, cowboy. I'll have to hold you to that one," she teased. It was a great way to get exercise and there were water pitchers everywhere for the thirsty dancers. Who knew line dancing could be so much fun?

Several songs later, she was exhausted. A few of the older folks danced off to the side, doing their own thing. The band played a slow song.

"I'm going to sit this one out," Mandy said.

"Or you could dance with me," Ben countered, taking her by the hand and pulling her close.

"Oh, I don't know. Sylvia might not want to be left alone," Mandy said, glancing down at her daughter.

Sylvia rolled her eyes. "Good grief, I'm not six. I want to go meet those kids over there," she said, pointing to a group of girls on the other side of the room.

"Those girls go to Pineview Elementary, which is where you'll start school in the fall, so I think that's a fabulous idea." Mandy said. It would take some getting used to letting Sylvia out of her sight, but she was trying. Her overprotectiveness had subsided a little, but she had a long way to go. "Jenna, will you keep an eye on Sylvia for me, please? Maybe give her some space, but make sure she's okay."

"Of course. Now the man asked you to dance...so dance," Jenna teased, giving her a light push toward the dance floor.

Ben took her by the hand and led her the rest of the way. He stepped in close and took her in his arms. She laid her head on his shoulder as they moved in time with the music. Soft and romantic, the melody wrapping around them like a warm embrace.

"I love you, Mandy," he whispered against her ear, his voice rough with emotion.

"I love you too, Captain Ben Calhoun." The title still made her smile, but not as much as the man who wore it.

"One day soon, I'm going to make you my wife." His words of promise made her heart skip.

"One day soon, you'll have to ask me first." Mandy grinned.

"You can count on it." Ben kissed her, soft and sweet just as the song ended.

They spotted Sylvia talking and laughing with her new friends, and Mandy let her continue, fighting the urge to hoover. It was good for all of them. *Especially Sylvia.*

As she watched her daughter bloom in this new life they were building, Mandy gave another prayer of gratitude. God had not only returned her daughter but had given her so much more—a second chance at love and happiness, a community that felt like family, and a future bright with promise.

Epilogue

EIGHTEEN MONTHS LATER...

The bright orange glow of sunset was brilliant through the kitchen window of the ranch house. Sylvia was carefully tearing apart the salad greens, cutting up the mushrooms and tomatoes and placing them in each bowl. The bag of croutons was ready for her to shake on top when she finished. The aroma of fresh-baked sourdough bread and pot roast filled the air as Mandy prepared dinner. She still couldn't believe all the changes in her life over the past year and a half.

True to his words, Ben had asked her to marry him just a month after that magical night at the community dance. He'd planned an evening under the stars, their special spot on the porch transformed with twinkling lights and flowers. When he dropped to one knee, Sylvia had appeared from her hiding spot with a handmade sign that read *Say Yes!*

Of course, she'd said yes, as there was never any doubt in her mind she wanted to marry Ben. Through the blur of tears, Ben slid his mother's engagement ring onto her finger. It was the most beautiful ring, with a small diamond in the middle and a circle of sapphires around it. Ben said it was the sea of love.

Pastor Phil presided over the wedding at the local church. It was a sunset ceremony with their closest friends and lots of folks from town in attendance. Turned out, a few squawking gossips didn't represent the townsfolk overall opinion of Ben, and they had welcomed him home with open arms and hearts.

Jenna had been Mandy's maid of honor, with Sylvia as the most beautiful bridesmaid and Veronica's twin girls as flower girls. Chief Jackson had walked her down the aisle.

Ben's old boss and friend, Ranger Chief Wilcox was the best man, and Ethan, Veronica's son was a groomsman. The two kids were a perfect complement to each other. It had been a pleasure to finally meet Terrance, and interestingly enough, it appeared there might be a little romance starting between him and Jenna.

The real blessing came two months later when a pregnancy test showed positive. *Twins.* God certainly had a sense of humor.

Ben stayed busy, splitting his time between his duties as captain and working the ranch, which was slowly coming back to its former glory. There was even talk of adding a herd of cattle next spring and hiring some ranch hands to help. Over the past year and a half, he still assisted the Rangers with tracking down more of the children and bringing the criminals to justice. So far, five of the children were located, which was a huge blessing. And her husband wouldn't stop helping them until every one of the children were found.

Veronica and Mandy had become best friends, and she moved to Crossroads Creek. She was happier and found peace in her life, and Mandy continued to pray for her.

Sylvia tended the garden with Mandy, her daughter's surprising interest, a huge motivator to grow lots of vegetables. At ten and a half, her daughter was counting down the days until she was a pre-teen, while Mandy was begging for the days to slow down so that she could enjoy every precious second. At times, Mandy almost wished she had opted to stay home with her daughter, but she did love working as an assistant for Rebecca Wentworth, the local attorney in town.

Even Frieda had adjusted beautifully, appointing herself official protector of the twins and never straying far from their side.

"I love you, Mom," Sylvia said, after she had set the table for dinner.

Mandy never tired of hearing those words. "I love you too, sweetheart."

"You know what else I love?" Sylvia asked, her eyes sparkling with the same joy that hadn't dimmed since the twins' arrival.

"What's that?" She smiled at her daughter, loving these moments they shared. These quiet conversations in the kitchen had become their special time, a chance to connect and share their hearts.

"That I finally have a brother and sister," Sylvia said, her voice soft with wonder.

"Yes, Lisa and Larry are a dream come true for all of us. I just know you'll be the best big sister ever," Mandy said, hugging her daughter close as they watched Ben playing with the twins, who were just starting to crawl. Lisa was already trying to push herself up to stand, while Larry was content to crawl everywhere.

Jenna was wrong. Blessings didn't come in threes. In her life, they just kept coming. The return of her precious daughter. Finding love with Ben. The birth of their beautiful twins. Frieda's joyful addition to the family. The peace that filled their home. It all added up to show that God's faithfulness had proven greater than the trials either of them had faced.

As Mandy pulled the bread from the oven, she sent up a silent prayer of thanksgiving. This was more than just a happy ending; it was a beautiful beginning, a testimony to God's perfect plan, written in the language of love and family. One day, her daughter might want to know the truth of the past, but for now, this blessing was more than enough.

"Dinner's ready!" she called out, and the answering chorus of voices —from Ben's deep rumble to the twins' excited squeals, to Frieda's excited barking...it was all the sweetest music Mandy had ever heard.

***

If you enjoyed this sweet and charming romance, be sure to check out the ALSO BY ELSIE DAVIS section on the next page for more clean and wholesome romance.

Next up – Book 7 – The Life of a Cowboy

Want to keep in touch with new releases and what's happening in the world of Elsie Davis? Sign up for the monthly newsletter at Elsie Davis.com

The greatest compliment you could give an author is to leave a review in order to help other readers discover the same great stories you enjoyed. Amazon/Bookbub/Goodreads are all great places. Many thanks!!!
Another great way to keep in touch - *Follow Elsie Davis on FaceBook*

Also By Elsie Davis

Sweet, Clean, and Wholesome Stories...with a Happily-Ever-After Guarantee!

Great Smoky Mountain Getaways
(Christian Inspirational – Women's Fiction Romances)
Juliet's Journey to Love
Poppy's Path to Love
Rachel's Road to Love
Taylor's Trek to Love
Grace's Getaway to Love – TBA
Dixie's Detour to Love – TBA
Angel's Adventure to Love – TBA

Crossroads Creek Cowboys
(Christian Inspirational Romances)
The Heart of a Cowboy
The Help of a Cowboy
The Return of a Cowboy
The Care of a Cowboy
The Dream of a Cowboy
The Tears of a Cowboy
The Life of a Cowboy – TBA

Holidays in Hallbrook
(Sweet Romance Series for Holidays
Throughout the Year)
***Welcome to Hallbrook, New Hampshire. A
small-town filled with the unexpected, lots
of love, and of course, a beloved dog to ramp
up the excitement.***
Love & Order (Labor Day)
Love & Family (Thanksgiving)
Love & Peace (Christmas)
Love & Chocolate (Valentine's Day)
Love & Hope (Mother's Day)
Love & Liberty (Independence Day)

Love & Honor (Veteran's Day)
Love & Joy (Easter)
Love & Adventure (Father's Day)
Lov & Cheer (New Year's Day – TBA)

Sundancer's Legacy

(Contemporary Christian Romance)

Sundancer's Star
Sundancer's Joy
Sundancer's Majesty – TBA

Planned Books in Series – TBA
Sundancer's Heart
Sundancer's Miracle
Sundancer's Glory
Sundancer's Kiss
Sundancer's Moon
Sundancer's Splendor

Trinity River Romances
(Sweet Western Romance)
Ranchers and farmers depend on the Trinity River for water, but when a secret conglomerate starts buying up property by fair means or foul, it's time for the landowners of Tumble County to fight back—Texas style. But what they don't count on, is finding love in the process.
Back in the Rancher's Arms
Small Town, Big Secrets
The Firefighter's Miscalculation – TBA
Love Advice for the Cowboy – TBA

Crestfield Inn Romances
If you like special kinds of soulmates, a splash of the supernatural, and wholesome relationships, you'll adore this sweet bit of fun filled with romance and mystery.
Turning Back Time
Turning Up Roses
Turning Down Pie

Celebrity Corgi Romance
(Standalone Sweet Romance/Light Mystery)
If you like light mystery mixed in with your happily-ever-after, you'll enjoy this second-chance romance and the race to save an adorable Corgi.
Digging the Driver

Gold Coast Retrievers
(Standalone Sweet Romance/Light Mystery)
Special Golden Retrievers help their humans solve mysteries, save lives, and even find love...
Defending Dakota

About The Author

Elsie Davis is a *USA Today and International Bestselling Author* of over 30 sweet, clean, and wholesome romances, and a member of the ACFW. She discovered the world of Happily-Ever-After romance at the age of twelve when she began avidly reading Barbara Cartland, the Queen of Romance, and has been hooked ever since. After building her dream log home on top of a small mountain, she turned her attention to do what she loves most, writing. Elsie writes sweet Contemporary Romance and Contemporary Christian Romance from her heart...hoping to share a little love in a big world.

When she's not writing, she can be found birding, kayaking, camping, fishing, playing disc golf, and taking nature walks—hoping to spot wildlife. Basically, she loves all things outdoors, EXCEPT cold weather. She and her husband are avid Caribbean cruisers, but Elsie's favorite vacation was their cruise to Alaska. (In spite of the cold!) Indoors, she enjoys a toasty fire, and of course, a great romance with a guaranteed Happily-Ever-After.

https://www.elsiedavis.com